IMPERFECT MURDERER'S DIARY

The Criminalist

Manuel Tovar

PROLOGUE

It is common for the prologue to be written by someone else, but due to unforeseen circumstances, I have had to improvise and ask my other self to assist me in this purpose. The fundamental reasons for writing this book were several: first, for readers to enjoy a pleasant reading experience, even when discussing sex or intimate situations so that the reader does not feel offended by explicit language or obscene situations. I wanted them to feel comfortable and attracted to the romantic details of the situations, while at the same time feeling the need to set a good example for their children. This would help them in fostering a healthy youth and adulthood, and consequently, a positive view of their parents, the righteousness of the father, and the honesty of the mother.

Additionally, I aimed for this work to serve as inspiration for those who doubt their intellectual capabilities or find themselves in poverty, so that they realize that, with sacrifice and dedication, even the most challenging dreams can be achieved. This is the story of Alexis, who, despite his trauma and the precariousness of his beginnings, managed to fulfill the purpose he had set in his mind.

I also want to express my gratitude to the people who have given me encouragement and love to achieve what took some time but, with their motivation, I managed to fulfill my dream. I refer to Manny, Mónica, Jessica, Thelma, Ninett, and especially to God, who granted me health and inspiration to carry out what is now yours.

Chapter I

My two victims gaze at me with nostalgia, missing the beauty of life from the place where the departed rest, where there is no choice but to look without being seen, to hear without being heard, and to scream without being listened to. To patiently await the day when they will be held accountable by the creator and wait for their executioner to join them in penance. Meanwhile, I will continue doing what pleases me the most—remembering them in the beautiful form they had when they inhabited this world as human beings, with all their physical, spiritual, intellectual, and other qualities. Regretting that they had to depart prematurely, when they were in the prime of youth, with a bright future awaiting them due to their culture and brilliant intellectual qualities, when they were the joy of their parents and everyone around them, including myself.

It all began like this... I was a very polite and diligent child, in my second year of elementary school. On that day, due to the twists of fate, classes ended abruptly because of our teacher's health issue. All students of the same grade were sent home, but due to the responsibility instilled in me by my parents, I didn't stay to play with my classmates. On the contrary, I hurried to get home with the idea of helping my mother with some household chores, hoping for a piece of the delicious apple pie she had made the day before as a reward.

I was very excited, kicking small stones I found on the side of the road. In my tender imagination, all kinds of beings filled my dreams, making me daydream and transporting me to fantastical worlds. I imagined flying on winged steeds, just like the ones in the fairy tales I read during my many leisure hours. I also dreamed of winged maidens who, taking me by the hand, transported me to enormous and beautiful castles where I met opulent kings and princesses who praised me with delicious feasts. I played in their beautiful and vast gardens filled with the most varied and beautiful flowers, all while their sons and daughters were attended to by diligent pages who offered us all kinds of drinks and snacks.

I continued walking, paying little attention to the few people and vehicles that traversed the nearly deserted streets leading to our house. It was a beautiful house with an acre of land, adorned with a lovely brick-colored fence, a shed, and a garage for two cars. Two beautiful oak trees provided shade in the summer and protection from the rain in winter. The house's facade was painted in a soft yellow, with brown window frames and door colors. The interior comprised three bedrooms, a living room, a dining room, and a laundry room in the backyard. The slightly darker brown roof served as a playground for mischievous squirrels, providing a pleasant distraction in the otherwise monotonous area.

My mother, Jennifer, didn't work outside the home. Her special task was taking care of the household, my younger brother (David), and me. Additionally, she attended to my father, R.R. (named after the famous President Ronald Reagan), who spent most of his time working as a manager at the town's hardware store. There was a lady who helped with laundry on weekends so that my mother could focus on taking care of my brother and me, as well as attending to my father when he returned hungry in the evenings and other matters that only they understood and that didn't concern me at all. My mother had an old SUV that she used for weekly grocery shopping and to pick up my father when his Buick occasionally broke down.

They were well-liked in the area but didn't have many friends, except for Charles, who was supposedly my father's best friend. They usually got together on Sundays to have a few beers, enjoy a football game, play some card games, and talk about the small happenings in the town. We lived in North Sarasota, Florida, and had a very peaceful life until that day that would be marked by destiny—the day that would be the stigma in my mind for many years.

I remember my father being tall, maybe about six feet, strong as a bull, with an energetic yet sincere gaze. I don't recall him speaking ill of anyone, and he always preferred to settle any differences personally. He didn't yell, but he had a resonant and well-accented voice. His favorite sport was splitting wood with his axe. My mother was also tall, maybe around five-ten, fair-skinned with blond and wavy hair. Her face reminded me of one of those mythological goddesses seen in movies. Looking at her photograph, the only thing I managed to keep close to me, along with her meticulous care, especially in my personal grooming, as she was very particular about my attire and personal hygiene, paying special attention to my always impeccable hairstyle.

"I had stopped at the entrance of the house and stood there watching the squirrels. It seemed like my subconscious was warning me that something was happening, and it would be best not to be a witness, that I should wait for everything to pass before entering my house. I should let time go by, entertaining myself with something that kept my tender mind focused on the fantasies that made me a happy child. However, what had to happen happened. Before entering the house, I cut a small yellow flower that I found along the way, thinking of surprising my mother with that little detail. So, opening the front door, I headed to the living room, expecting to find my mother checking the mail or knitting while my little brother slept, and later going to the kitchen to prepare a snack for both of us. However, she wasn't there. I went to the kitchen and didn't find her either. I peeked into the backyard, thinking she might be hanging laundry or taking out the trash, but she wasn't there either. My last resort was her bedroom, so that's where I headed. The door was closed, but I could hear noises... so I decided to open it to see what was going on, driven by my natural childhood curiosity."

When I opened the door I exclaimed excitedly: hello mommy" waiting surprise her with my anticipated arrival and carrying the little flower in my hand, I was the one surprised because she didn't even hear me, she was like in a trance, suffocated, making strange sounds, as if she were going crazy with his head back and pulling his hair, I still remember that he said more, more, more, and moaned and sobbed, I stayed standing in the door frame without knowing what was happening, suddenly the one downstairs who was "daddy's best friend"He raised his head and when he saw me he told my mother, who turned her head. face and making a face of madness and anger, he ordered me to go to the room and that she would arrive right away.

I obeyed the order, a little confused, and sat on the couch waiting for Mom to arrive. Of course, she took her time, and now I understand why. She had to finish her orgasm and compose herself to talk to me. Besides, she had to think about what to say and be convincing. She came out alone; supposedly, Charles had left through the bedroom window to avoid the embarrassment of facing me and having nothing to say. However, my mother had already figured out what to tell me, and she began like this: "Look, son, you're too young to understand adult matters, but when you grow up, you'll understand. The important thing is not to tell your dad anything because he might get sick, and since you love him so much, I know you wouldn't want anything bad to happen to him, right?"

The truth is, I didn't understand anything, but since she told me not to say anything, I stayed silent... and so time passed. A few weeks later, by coincidence, my teacher fell ill again, and we were sent home once more. Sensing something bad, I didn't want to get home quickly, but I also thought that if I didn't arrive on time, I might receive a scolding from my mom. So, I headed home as quickly as possible and entered quietly, hoping to find everything normal. However, the same thing happened; I couldn't find her anywhere. This time, I took care to open the door to her bedroom just a little... finding the same scene as before. It was frustrating for my young age, but I didn't have enough judgment to intervene and defend the honor of our home and the tarnishing of my father's name.

Faced with the impossibility of doing anything about it, I began to lose my appetite, experiencing nightmares and sleeplessness. This prompted my mother to take me to the doctor, though before anything else, she ordered me not to tell anything about what I had seen, as otherwise, my father would also have to see a doctor. I promised and kept my word. The doctor prescribed some natural relaxants and suggested taking me to the beach to soak up the sun for a quick recovery with a change of activities. Although both she and I knew the reason for my illness, they took me to the beach for a couple of days. Even at my young age, I tried to get used to the idea that I would keep the secret until I could do something about it.

And so time passed until I had a better understanding. I was already ten years old and in fourth grade. I had grown quite a bit since then, and although I was still reserved, my character was stable. There had been no more unpleasant encounters involving my mother and Charles, so I assumed they had ended their relationship. Thus, there was no offense to pursue. Even though I understood that what they had done was wrong and harmful to my father, I tried to focus on my studies and playing with my little brother, who had also grown and made a good companion.

On that day, as usual, I went to school early. Upon arrival, I found out that a child had chickenpox, so they didn't let us enter the classrooms. Instead, they requested the health department to come for a children's inspection and impose a quarantine. After examining each of us, they allowed us to go home with a note of care instructions and a future notice about the resumption of classes. So, I headed home again around ten in the morning.

When I arrived, I tried to make as much noise as possible, but since my little brother was in his nap time, I had to refrain from making any noise. I went straight to my mom's bedroom, and when I knocked on her door, she answered all hysterically, "Go to the living room and don't bother; we'll talk later because I'm getting dressed." I went to the backyard to dissipate my annoyance at how she treated me. Suddenly, I saw the window of the bedroom opening, and Charles came out through it, still buttoning up his shirt and tightening his pants' belt. I watched him head towards the street behind our property, where he left his car during his encounters with my mom.

I would have wanted to be an adult and give him a piece of my mind, but unfortunately, I was just a child and didn't know what to do. However, that night, I would make one of the most significant decisions of my life. It would be the night that would completely transform my world. From that night on, nothing would be the same in the life of Alexis Bravo. It would be the last night I slept in a child's bed because starting the next day, I would become a man and not seek who owed me, but who would pay me back. I knew I had been a good kid, but from that night on, my entire future was about to be decided.

We are all born good, all innocent until the moment when our instincts are awakened, whether they be good or bad, through the examples provided to us or through their teachings. That's when we become saints or demons, when we pour out love or poison.

The next morning, at dawn, I grabbed my backpack and packed two complete changes of clothes along with the one I would wear. I knew nothing was going to be easy from then on. I broke my piggy bank and took out all my savings. It might have been around twenty dollars. It wasn't much, but it would serve me to eat while I found a place to do something to earn my daily sustenance. I couldn't continue witnessing something as depressing and traumatizing as my mom's dishonest actions. She didn't care about the respect she owed her husband, her children, and her self-respect, especially. She disregarded everything, only focusing on satisfying her sexual appetite without considering the consequences of the damage it caused to her home and the people who cared about her.

Perhaps by leaving, I was punishing her, making her feel responsible for whatever might happen to me. Or, on the contrary, I might have been making it easier for her by removing a witness to her misguided actions. Perhaps my departure could push her to make an effort to change her behavior and focus on loving my father or to leave him once and for all. Of course, these were the thoughts of a child about to turn eleven. I had no experience in matters of love and sex, but I already had a grasp of common sense. Therefore, I could discern when something was wrong and when it was right. However, no one would take into account the opinions of a child. So, what I thought or didn't think was out of the question. I packed my things and left. I didn't know where to go, but I did what birds do—I flew south.

Charlotte was a densely populated place with many opportunities for employment. However, I arrived very tired due to the journey I made in the back of a cargo truck, where I had hitchhiked. So, I headed to a fast-food restaurant with the idea of grabbing something to eat to regain my strength. Later, I would find a place to spend the approaching harsh night. Despite everything, the weather was dry and hot, so I wasn't concerned about sleeping under any bridge or in a garage without doors.

There was an elderly homeless man rummaging through garbage bins, trying to find something to eat. Since I was new to the streets, I asked him, "What are you looking for?" He replied, "Food, son, food," and continued sifting through papers and cardboard cups with drink residues. I felt sorry for the poor man and asked him if he fancied a hamburger. He looked at me very surprised and asked, "Do you have enough to treat me to one?" I nodded and asked him to follow me.

I ordered two cheeseburgers, fries, and two medium drinks. Then, I invited the man to sit with me. Very surprised, he said, "I think you have a good heart, but it's better that when you do something like this, you pay attention to who you invite. There are too many people who aren't good in this world, and some, out of gratitude, can rob or harm you. Be careful with whom you talk to, okay?" "Alright," I replied. "Thanks... I won't forget it."

After enjoying the meal, I asked for his name. "Daniel," he said, and I told him mine. The man couldn't understand how a child my age was alone and had struck up a conversation with a homeless old man. Nevertheless, he promised to help me in whatever way he could and teach me all the survival tricks of the street. However, he advised me that it would be best to return home after I had told him about my escape, but without mentioning the reasons.

And so began a friendship that would last for a few years. I learned some survival tricks, such as how to ask people for money, as no one wanted to give me a job due to my age and the penalties for employing minors. However, it turned out that my old friend was a very educated person; he was a doctor who had lost his license due to malpractice resulting from his alcohol problem. Although, as he told me, the reality had been that it was a revenge against the hospital director who had offended him. "Anyway," my friend would say, "I needed a break."

After getting what we needed for the day, we would move to a wooded area to contemplate the purposes of life, to understand that things happen for a reason. "Look," he'd say, "if you hadn't run away from home, you wouldn't be keeping company with an old, lonely, and melancholic man, whom you brighten the days with your presence. In return, I teach you everything about biology and other sciences I studied at university in the field of medicine. You'll learn to heal yourself and use folk remedies for serious health problems."

We had secured a small room in a house on the outskirts of the city, so the most basic need was solved. We acquired furniture that more privileged people discarded, allowing us to furnish our little room. We painted it appropriately with leftover paint that we were once paid to dispose of. With this paint, we achieved a beautiful shade of blue that, according to my friend and now teacher, provided us with a good amount of energy and motivation.

He was a good teacher; in a few months, he had turned me into a math whiz, and I had made significant progress in biology. By that time, I was already fourteen years old. It seemed like it had been yesterday, but in reality, more than three years had passed. I missed everyone, but I harbored great resentment against my mother. Therefore, I preferred to focus on something else rather than think about her.

My voice had started to change, so my teacher and friend warned me about the hormonal changes happening in my body, along with other common transformations. He also cautioned me about instincts awakening in a person as they entered puberty. It was something normal but had certain reactions that sometimes altered the mood in both boys and girls. He emphasized that every issue had its solutions at its specific time.

Therefore, he suggested I start an exercise program, at least five days a week. This would help me build a strong and athletic body, as well as divert my attention from any other natural problems that might arise.

And a new rhythm of life began. We had no hurry, and life was meant to be lived in the best way or however one felt was best. With my help, we had managed to change our lifestyle. He contributed his wisdom, and I brought my strength and youth. We made a good team, and everything improved day by day. My friend, who initially couldn't do without alcohol daily, had become a staunch teetotaler. With the money saved from not buying liquor, we purchased healthy food and treated ourselves to the luxury of going to the cinema occasionally. Moreover, we no longer begged or scavenged for leftover food. We were poor but dignified citizens, and time passed.

Between occasional jobs, collecting recyclable materials, and occasional donations from neighbors and friends we had made, we lived a normal life. However, my sexual awakening was just around the corner, and something very ugly for me would begin there. It was my disdain for women that frustrated my affection for them. I liked them, but I felt a contempt for them due to the trauma caused by my mother.

Chapter II

I felt frustrated because I desired them, but at the same time, the memory of my mother's infidelity came to mind, and I thought that all women were the same, that they all deserved to be punished because deep down, sooner or later, they would do the same. So, I was in that emotional conflict that confused me and unconsciously pushed me away from them, even though at my age, with my masculine demeanor, and with my physical appearance that wasn't entirely unpleasant, there was the occasional girl who wanted to give me a chance. I was afraid or embarrassed to ask my old friend. Besides, I didn't want to cause him problems because his health had started to deteriorate due to his age and the alcoholic life he had led for some years.

On that cold winter morning, everything dawned purple-lipped and with a persistent cough. As I approached his rickety little bed, I could see he was trembling intensely from the cold. I prepared a hot tea and placed it in his hands while urging him to go to the hospital. "I'm fine," he said, pretending to be okay, but I didn't believe him at all. Taking his hand and putting an old coat on him, I lifted him from the bed and helped him walk to the door. He couldn't stand on his own, so after laying him back in bed, I went to the owners of the small room, pleading with them to call 911, hoping an ambulance would soon arrive to take him to the hospital. "The ambulance is coming," I said, "you'll get better soon, and we'll continue the business. I have plans... so get ready. I'll keep an eye on your health and visit you during your stay there."

In the distance, the ambulance siren could be heard, its ominous wail foretelling something I wouldn't have liked to anticipate. Upon hearing it, he became downcast and contemplative. With a melancholic tone, he said to me, "I know what I have, and I don't think I'll live much longer. What saddens me the most is that now that I've met you, my desire to live had increased. I thought God had sent me the son I never had and always dreamed of. I have had a savings account for a while, and a few days ago, out of the affection I have for you, I included you in it. I just hope you give me a decent burial and start a new life when you're alone. I couldn't hold back my tears and tenderly hugged him, telling him he wouldn't die, that the doctors would make him better and everything would be the same or better than before. I asked him to have faith and put all his effort into recovering. We were talking when the ambulance arrived, and they placed him on the stretcher. He took my hand and said before leaving, 'May God protect you, and I'll be watching over you from the place I'm about to go to very soon.' And they took him away. I stood at the doorstep, feeling more alone than a man on a deserted island, and I cried like I had never cried before. After my tears had stopped, I promised myself that no one would ever be a reason for me to cry again.

I knew I couldn't withdraw any money from the bank until I was of legal age, but I still held onto the hope that he would be healed in the hospital and that we would soon be together again. However, I was determined to keep my promise no matter what.

I got myself together and headed to where they would likely have admitted him. Upon arrival and inquiring about his name, I was informed that he was in intensive care. I had to wait for more comprehensive information because he was in a restricted area at that moment. I prayed to God for his healing and promised to always be a good person, hoping that would somehow aid in his quick recovery. I also thought he deserved a chance, similar to the opportunities he had given to so many people whom he had healed through his medical expertise. That day, I didn't go looking for a job; instead, I inquired about him every hour, hoping for good news that would make me feel better.

The entire day passed into night. I imagined he was fighting for his life, hoping that his will to live would be stronger than any virus or bacteria that might harm him. My hope was pinned on my prayers and his courage to fight, just as he had fought against life's injustices.

Al approaching the information desk the next morning, an older nurse asked me if I was related to the patient. I lied and said I was his son, insisting on knowing about his condition. She inquired about my mother, as any information had to be given to an adult. I told her we were alone and that I was motherless, leaving her looking distressed and unsure of what to say. Suddenly, with a mix of tenderness and sadness, she told me, "Your father passed away and will soon be transferred to the morgue. An adult can arrange for cremation or transfer to a funeral home. Call a relative or friend for help with the formalities. If preferred, call this number; it's from a very good funeral home with reasonable prices," extending her hand with a card in it.

I was left speechless, unable to even muster the courage to say thank you. I walked out onto the street dragging my feet as if each weighed a ton. My young mind couldn't figure out what to do or whom to turn to. All I could think was that I was alone and that no one could fill the void left by that wonderful man who had connected with me better than if he had been my own father. Surprisingly, the idea of calling the funeral home recommended by the nurse at the hospital came to mind. I took some coins from my pocket, dialed the number on the card, and waited for someone to answer.

Ring, ring, "Hello, Sweet Remembrance Funeral Home, how can I help you?"

My father passed away this morning, and I want to know what I need to do for you to give him a Christian burial."

First, you'll need to tell me the deceased's name, where he passed away, and what kind of service you prefer. Also, whether you'll be paying in cash, by credit card, or if you prefer a payment plan."

After inquiring about the most convenient service, I provided all the necessary information and promised to bring an advance payment later that afternoon to initiate the arrangements. After expressing gratitude and knowing the price, I headed towards our small room to begin executing my plan, which had only just started to take shape. The cost was two thousand dollars, and I wanted to know how much we had in our small cash box. We had paid the rent about three days ago, so rent wasn't a concern for the moment. I entered the room and went straight to the shoebox we used as a safe, emptied it out, and began counting. Between coins and bills, we had a hundred and eighty... so, we were short by a thousand eight hundred twenty. It seemed like an insurmountable amount, but I was determined to gather it one way or another.

I searched for one of the empty paint cans we had in a corner of the room and made a slit in the lid to turn it into a collection jar. I prepared to gather donations from everyone who knew us. Before heading out, I made a stop at the landlady's house to inform her of the news and let her know that I would be in charge from then on. "Don't worry, and I'm very sorry for what happened," she said. "What's that jar for?" That's when I told her about my plan. It was then I realized that the lady wasn't as harsh as she seemed, as she immediately asked me to wait while she went to her living room and returned with the first donation of a hundred dollars.

I began my journey hoping people would generously contribute. Everyone was kind and gave according to their means, but I was far from gathering even half of the total. By five in the evening, I had only managed to collect nine hundred dollars. However, as the most crucial thing was to leave a deposit, I went to the funeral home with what I had. I would try to get the rest the next day.

When I arrived, the man who attended me was surprised and asked if there was an adult in charge. I explained that I was handling things and, when it came to responsibility, I was as capable as an adult. I placed the nine hundred dollars I had on the counter. The man counted the money and gave me a receipt, assuring me that the body would be at the funeral home for the wake that same night. With no desire to return to the small room, I told the man I would wait there until my father arrived to be mourned.

It was new and disheartening for me to sit in front of the coffin of someone I had learned to love like a true father. However, I no longer felt the urge to cry. On the contrary, it comforted me to remember the happy moments we had despite our poverty and age difference. I cherished memories of his patience in teaching me logic and math problems, reviewing my anatomy lessons, the tests he prepared for me in biology or chemistry, and his insistence that I study works in psychology (Sigmund Freud), philosophy (Socrates, Plato, Confucius), and history (where we mentally traveled to the most remote places and times), imaginatively enjoying beautiful places and fantastic events.

Being lost in my thoughts, a very elegant man accompanied by an equally refined lady appeared at the door of the funeral parlor. With a deeply mournful expression, they approached me and asked who I was. For a moment, I remained silent, not understanding why it mattered to them who I was. Breaking out of my confusion, I stood up and told them I was the deceased's son, asking who they were and why they were asking. Both replied in unison: "My uncle never had children," said the lady. "My brother didn't have children," affirmed the man. "Yes, I know," I responded, "but he wanted me to be the son he never had, and we almost made it. We cared for each other as if it were so. Besides, he's there if you want to pay your respects, and then you can leave... because I'm fulfilling his last wish, to have a Christian burial."

Come on, don't be upset, we want to help with whatever is needed," they said. "Who paid to take him out of the hospital?" they continued. "That's not important," I replied. "What matters is praying for his soul's rest and giving him a proper burial, tomorrow or whenever possible." The funeral home employee had made some arrangements to prepare the body and had dressed him in a collared shirt, tie, and suit jacket, looking quite dignified. The lady approached the casket and, looking through the glass, couldn't hold back her tears. "Why didn't you take care of yourself, uncle? Why didn't you come back home to be happy with us?" she sobbed, as if she wished my dear friend could hear her.

I also approached to gaze at his face once more before I wouldn't have that chance anymore. He seemed asleep, and I thought it was because of the contentment of having been an honest and sincere man, of not wishing ill on anyone and accepting life's paths with humility. The brother had stepped out momentarily, probably to talk to the funeral home employee and take care of the remaining matters.

I thought I was surplus, so after looking at him with the tenderness of a son towards his father, I began to leave without saying anything, with the belief that the family would take care of whatever was left, ensuring that the essence of his final wish would be fully honored. I had done what I could, and God was my witness. I thought I had fulfilled my promise and would try to continue my life as usual, as my friend Daniel had advised me. I was already out the door of the funeral home when suddenly I felt someone grab my arm and, pulling me, said, "You can't leave, I need to talk to you for a moment. First, I have to thank you for what you did for my brother. Second, tell me about his last days and whether he ever spoke of us."

After sitting face to face, I started to tell him in detail about our friendship and how we met, although I omitted the detail of searching for food in bins and the invitation I extended. I was honest in saying that my friend had never spoken to me about his family and preferred to focus on any other topic, although I knew he had a diary in which he mysteriously wrote details of each day. He asked me to rest and come the next day, when we would lay him to rest in the family plot, and pleaded for me to bring the aforementioned diary if I happened to find it. He also mentioned that the funeral home owner would refund the deposit I had given and that I could do as I saw fit with it. I insisted it wasn't necessary, but the man wasn't one to plead; he commanded. So, I had no choice but to accept, although I would later decide how to invest it in something related to the passing of my great friend, mentor, and adoptive father.

I went back to the small room to try to rest, although I knew it would be nearly impossible. Nonetheless, I tried to at least relax and prepare myself to look presentable for the next day, which would be our final farewell. I woke up early, took a shower, had some food, and headed to the funeral home to await the hour of our parting, with the promise to meet again in the afterlife after my departure. I had found the book in which my friend wrote his most important daily events, and I carried it with me. After greeting the elegant gentleman, I handed it to him, asking that he keep it safe, which he agreed to do. The lady, Doris, appeared a few minutes later and, greeting me, said, "My name is Doris, and yours?" I replied dryly, "Alexis," not knowing what else to say. We remained silent for a while until she spoke again: "We want you to come with us in our car because you were very important to my uncle, and we also want to be your friends."

The burial passed amid tears from me and some who loved him, including Doris and her brother, who discreetly wiped the tears from his eyes. After the attendees said their goodbyes and flowers were placed—arriving late for the ceremony—before I could bid farewell, Doris asked me to allow them to take me home so they could know where to find me if they had anything to tell me. Additionally, she gave me her father's (the elegant gentleman) business card, urging me not to hesitate to call if I needed anything or remembered something about her uncle that I considered relevant. Despite feeling great sadness due to the depressing place where we lived, I had no choice but to accept. We left immediately, and on the way, I asked if they wanted to keep the books Daniel had left in the apartment, which they declined. On the contrary, the elegant gentleman encouraged me to read them, unaware that I had already gone through them several times in my eagerness to intellectually improve myself.

Mr. Bill was his name, an affluent businessman who, due to special circumstances, had never assisted his brother. He was reluctant to accept any kind of help, striving to be a free man, unburdened by any ties and indebted to no one, not even to his own family. Before leaving, Mr. Bill said to me, "I hope you don't move from here, at least until I figure out how I can help you. You seem like a smart young man with potential. Give me about two or three days, and you'll hear from me through my chauffeur, who will come to see you." And they departed, with a friendly smile from Doris, who waved goodbye as the car disappeared into the distance. It left me with an indescribable feeling throughout my being, something like butterflies in the stomach and a chill down my spine. Was it hormones going crazy, or did I feel something called an attraction to the opposite sex?

It was a beautiful blonde, she would have been at most sixteen years old and was very lovely, maybe around my height, with beautiful curly hair, blue eyes with long eyelashes, well-groomed thick eyebrows, tiny ears "tiny and well-shaped, her face was finished with a perky little nose and a beautiful mouth with thick, red, and sensual lips, adorned with a perfect set of teeth. Her body was like that of a seasoned athlete; not even a gram of fat was noticeable. Her beautiful breasts seemed to be made of granite, just like her well-rounded buttocks. She was very young, but due to my knowledge of anatomy, I could easily discern the qualities or attributes of a woman."

In a few days, I would turn fifteen, feeling older, perhaps due to my experiences with life, my premature maturity stemming from the wealth of knowledge I had acquired, and my continuous hard work. I had little interaction with people my age, which deprived me of a normal childhood. Nevertheless, I felt like a grown man and could sense Doris's affection towards me. However, returning to reality, I realized there was an abyss between her and me, separating us like the Earth from the moon. I needed to make plans for the next day's work because surely dreams don't provide food or pay rent. Moreover, I had to do what my friend had advised me: keep improving myself to become someone in life."

So passed the three days that Mr. Bill had asked for me to think about how to help myself. Truthfully, I wasn't interested in his help; I had what I wanted and knew how to earn my daily living. However, thoughts of Doris' attributes crossed my mind again, and I thought that if his help gave me the chance to see her again, then accepting it might be okay, as long as her father's offer was genuine. It was the third day, but I still spent my time cleaning a couple of yards (backyards). After that, I collected some recyclable materials (aluminum cans and plastic bottles), which I sold before returning home. I was tired because I had started doing the work alone; my partner who used to help was no longer around. I missed him a lot, not for what he did, but for what his presence represented, providing support and educating me all the time.

After getting home, I took a bath and was preparing something to eat when I heard a knock at the door. 'Who is it?' I asked from the old stove. 'It's me, Mr. Bill's driver,' they answered from outside, and I immediately went to open the door."

What a great surprise to see Doris in front of me, accompanied by her driver. I greeted them both and invited them in, but they declined, mentioning they were in a hurry. They said they'd accept the invitation another day; the most important thing was that Mr. Bill wanted to speak with me the following day at ten in the morning, not a minute later, as he was a very busy man who valued punctuality. After delivering the message, they left. Before leaving, I heard the promise from Doris's beautiful lips that she would see me the next day at her house. She asked if I remembered the address, and I pulled out the card her father had given me from my pants pocket. 'See you tomorrow then,' she said.

I stood in the doorway until they had left, and Doris kept waving goodbye with her hand until they disappeared around the curve of the street, just like the last time."

"You finished cooking and ate the food without even knowing its taste. My heart had returned to its normal rhythm after they had left, and my hands no longer sweated as they did when she was in front of me, her beautiful face and the depth of her gaze, which seemed to read how much I admired her. At times, I felt the presence of memories of my mother, but I wanted to set aside that bitter memory to not tarnish the image of an earthly Angel, the embodiment of Aphrodite, or Helen of Troy. Perhaps the simplicity and magnificence of a fairy tale fairy or the perfection of the female human being. The truth was her physical beauty had no comparison, nor did the tenderness and sublimity of her soul, the melodiousness of her voice, and the sincerity of her gaze. She was like a virgin who had the mission to make me her most fervent devotee, someone who would transform solely for the privilege of seeing her every day.

I went to sleep after listening to some romantic melodies on an old radio we had on the bedside table, the same radio I used to listen to with my old friend, but now I listened to it alone. I tried to forget many pleasant memories of our time together (for now) and instead remember those wonderful blue eyes and Doris's sweet gaze, which made me float in the sea of illusions, pushed by the currents of dreams and struck by the waves of reality."

I slept with Doris's image in my mind; I wanted to dream while asleep as I did while awake. I wanted her image to be with me at any hour of the day or night. Even though I had many problems on my mind, her image served as relief, lightening my burdens. So, thinking and daydreaming like any boy my age, I fell asleep and didn't wake up until I felt the cold of the early morning, having dozed off in my clothes and shoes without properly bundling up.

Morning came, and I got up early as usual. The first thing I did was take a bath, then put on my best clothes and had a light meal. I wasn't hungry; I just felt a hollow feeling in my stomach and anxiety to know how Mr. Bill had thought of helping me. Although I hoped it wouldn't be something that took away my independence and ability to move, as that was what provided my happiness.

I arrived fifteen minutes before the agreed-upon time. It was a Saturday, and Doris was at the door, seemingly anxious from what I could tell. When she saw me, she stopped nervously wringing her fingers, relieved that I had come. 'I'm so glad you're here,' she said. 'I was afraid you wouldn't come because of your impulsive and reactionary nature, but I don't blame you... I imagine your life must be very tough and unsociable. Please don't be offended; my problem is that I always speak my mind.' 'Don't worry,' I said, 'my strength is in listening and responding if necessary, but it's just your opinion, and it's okay. I think you're right.'"

And suddenly, we had to stop talking upon hearing Mr. Bill's voice approaching the door, calling my name... 'Alexis...' he said. 'Come in; we need to talk, and I don't have all day.' I hurried and, after greeting him, took a seat in the chair in front of his desk. Despite my usual composure, I couldn't stop my slight trembling and the sweating of my hands.

Come on, don't worry, relax. This isn't a police interrogation, and all I want to know is if you have any projects in mind, something you'd like to do or a dream you'd like to fulfill.' I would have liked to tell him that my project was to finish my studies and marry Doris, but he wouldn't like that. So, I only mentioned finishing my studies and finding a suitable job. He looked at me inquisitively, and after a few minutes of analysis, he said, 'Well, I'll propose something to you. I want you to tell me if you'd like to come live at my house in one of the servant's quarters and attend a school that I would pay for, or live where you currently live, and I'll cover all the expenses, and all you have to do is study and bring me monthly reports from the school. Tell me what you prefer, or if you want to take your time, I'll give you the same three days I took to make this offer.'

I didn't have to think much. I knew that being there would give me the chance to see her every day, but I also thought that being there might distract me from the focus I needed for my studies. So, thanks to my mental agility, I replied, 'I'd like to continue living where I live, study, and bring you monthly reports on my progress. The only thing is, I don't know what grade I'd have to start in, because when I left school, I was in a grade relative to my age, but now I'm fifteen and have learned many things that might qualify me for a higher grade.'"

"Alright," he replied. "From now on, you won't have to worry about working as I'll cover the expenses for your house, rent, food. You'll attend a private school that I'll choose, ensuring it's accessible for you. My driver will take you to buy suitable clothes, and we'll make some adjustments to your apartment so that you feel comfortable. I'll also provide you with a monthly allowance for your personal expenses. I only ask that you don't spend on things that might harm your health or your future."

Chapter III

I had hired a teacher to conduct some assessments on me. After a series of tests, he provided a written recommendation for the school, suggesting the grade level at which I had the aptitude to continue my studies. Mr. Bill had already made arrangements with the school, paid all the necessary fees, and registered me as the son of my late friend. Therefore, my name was now Alexis Smith Siemens. It didn't sound bad at all; it gave me a certain elegance, and because it included my great friend's surname, I would try to honor it and live up to its reputation.

It had been worthwhile to dedicate so much time to studying, and thanks to the dedication of my tutor and teacher in educating me, I would only need to dedicate one more year to complete my high school. It wasn't bad at all, and I knew I would have the opportunity to see Doris, even if it were only once a month, or perhaps more..."

"I started on the right foot. Most of my classmates were older than me, but I had made a good impression on them, and everyone was helpful, at least being friendly and sharing their thoughts on topics of common interest. The change in my voice had become more noticeable, now sounding deeper, and I was starting to develop a tiny mustache, along with hair growing in various parts of my body. I felt a bit uncomfortable about the physical changes, but what worried me more were the morning erections that were occurring. I thought I might be getting sick with some rare illness. I no longer had my friend who might have helped and clarified my doubts. But then I remembered what he had once told me. I searched through the books he had left behind and found the answer. What was happening to me was logical, and all I had to do was control it and wait for the day when I'd have female company to practice my masculine instincts.

That's when memories of my mother's infidelity came to mind. I hoped I wouldn't have the opportunity to meet a woman who would trample on a good man's dignity, or one who would do to me what my mother did to my father.

A new phase of my life began. I no longer had to struggle to earn my daily living, waiting for someone to offer us odd jobs and pay us whatever they deemed fit. No longer did I have to endure the arrogance of those buying recyclable materials, treating me and other humble collectors disrespectfully, sometimes humiliatingly. Now, my only concern would be to study and achieve the best grades to keep my sponsor happy and continue supporting me. I aimed to improve intellectually, at least enough for Doris to take notice."

Deep down, I wished my mother had changed her ways, that my father remained the good man he always was, and that my little brother was growing up healthy, with the opportunities I was currently experiencing. I hoped to see them again one day, even if I might not feel any affection for my mother, perhaps only disdain for who she had been. Yet, I knew I could never claim anything from her simply because she was my mother.

So, I focused on my studies. I studied diligently, dedicatedly, and systematically, utilizing all the time I had and using my memory perfectly, becoming the top student in my class. I achieved first place in school, repaying Mr. Bill for his support with the immense satisfaction of the results and the personal satisfaction of not having failed in his project. I knew there would be more challenges ahead, and the real struggle was just beginning. However, I considered myself equipped to overcome the forthcoming challenges, especially after Mr. Bill's congratulations and Doris's heartfelt embrace, the best reward and greatest motivation.

After graduation, we shared a bit at the party. I didn't know how to dance, but it was delightful to be on the dance floor holding Doris's hand, moving our feet without any rhythm but never breaking eye contact. Later, the three of us enjoyed a delicious and elegant dinner, during which Mr. Bill asked me what was next. I replied, very excitedly, 'To keep learning. If you agree, I'd like to take summer classes in philosophy and the arts.' He thought it was perfect and authorized me to enroll and apply for a spot for the upcoming academic year—pre-university studies. Doris kept congratulating me, although for personal reasons, she studied at home with private tutors."

A month had passed since graduation, and I was already attending special classes. That afternoon, I decided to visit Doris under the pretext of delivering some rent receipts. When we were alone in her house's courtyard, knowing her father wasn't around yet (as he hadn't returned from his office), I had the idea to kiss Doris. I suddenly pulled her by the waist and kissed her abruptly (as I had never kissed before), but passionately. I poured all the love I felt for her into that kiss, and it felt like ambrosia from the gods. I felt her lips were heavenly. I felt like the happiest man in the world. She also felt something special, as I sensed her trembling in my arms. But instinctively, she abruptly pulled away and, looking at me firmly, said, 'You shouldn't have done that. You know well that we are not equals, and my being kind to you does not give you any rights. You are poor, and my father helps you, but you'll never be on our level, even if you acquire all the titles in the world. Never approach me again...' and she walked away into her house, leaving me stunned and speechless, watching that beautiful body vanish from my sight as she walked away.

I felt bewildered. My first reaction was to leave in a hurry, overwhelmed by a sense of guilt that consumed my soul. At the same time, I felt anger at her derogatory and humiliating comment. Moreover, I felt sorry, knowing what her father might say or do when he found out. Anyway, I went back to the small room where I lived and waited for whatever was to come. I had no other option. Three days passed, and nothing happened. I concluded that Doris hadn't said anything to her father. My love began to transform into vengeance due to the insult I had suffered. I devised a revenge strategy and started to execute it from that day. I knew she might have the richest man in the world, but not everyone is necessarily brilliant. I also knew that nobody could love her as I did. So, I decided to make her pay for what she had done. I focused on my studies, exercised intensely every day, and maintained a strict diet to attain an enviable physique. I avoided going to her house and waited for Mr. Bill's chauffeur, which had become a routine.

"The new school year at the Pre-University College began, and I started with the same enthusiasm and focus as always. Sometimes, I wouldn't sleep in my eagerness to learn everything I needed and more. I didn't hesitate to review the texts thoroughly to perfect my understanding of the subjects. I also compared notes with the most advanced students in the College to verify my learning. Additionally, I turned eighteen and became a true man. Though I attracted the attention of some of the most beautiful girls at the College, I didn't lose sight of my goal—to become a successful individual.

The year had passed, ending with outstanding grades. The College counselor suggested I continue my studies in Law school, stating that I had the potential to become a great lawyer. Thus, I continued my learning even during school breaks. After more than a year without seeing Doris, I received a call from Mr. Bill. He was surprised to see me and said, 'You've truly transformed into a real man.' Of course, I stood at six-foot-two, with a body sculpted like granite, strong and well-built. My hair had always been light brown, and my eyes were sky blue. A straight nose and medium-sized lips, along with a wide jaw, gave me that masculine and attractive touch. 'I called to congratulate you on the grades you sent through my chauffeur, but I don't understand why you've been absent from this house. You should have more contact with us to get to know influential people who could be a stepping stone in your career's success.'

I'll take that into account,' I said. We were in the middle of this when there was a sudden knock on the door. 'Come in,' said Mr. Bill, and in the doorway appeared Doris. She had also undergone an astonishing change, had grown a bit, and was more beautiful than before. She seemed like a true mythological goddess, although her haughtiness hadn't diminished. She was still as proud as ever, but I still cared for her. 'Hello, Doris,' I said, waiting for a response to my greeting. However, without any trace of insolence, she didn't bother acknowledging my greeting. I didn't take offense, but Mr. Bill immediately reacted, rejecting her disrespectful behavior and demanding good manners, representing the family's lineage. She immediately showed some annoyance and said, 'Hello, Mr. Alexis. I didn't hear you. Please forgive me... if you'll excuse me,' and left with a defiant gesture. Mr. Bill, a bit flustered, asked me to excuse her, to which I conciliatorily replied, 'Don't worry, Sir, we all have those difficult days sometimes.' Promising to visit them more often, I bid farewell and made my way to the exit."

I was crossing the garden to reach the exit when Doris appeared in front of me, flushed with anger. In a challenging tone, she said, 'Don't you think you're old and big enough to pay for your own studies and expenses instead of causing problems for my father?' I had always been very calm and preferred to avoid any argument, but that day was an exception. Looking straight at her in a wide challenge, I said, 'I don't know what your problem is, but I assure you that all I'm doing is pleasing your father. He deserves respect and obedience. His insistence that I dedicate myself exclusively to studying is because he's set out to do for someone else what he hasn't been able to do with his own daughter, who flatters herself, believing she deserves everything without making any sacrifice. But if that satisfies you, I'll tell your father that I won't accept his help anymore, and I'll leave your lives forever.' I began my return to Mr. Bill's office/study, and unintentionally, he had noticed the argument as he tried to catch up with me to give me the tuition check. He didn't say anything until he saw me heading inside. 'There's always a reason for everything,' he said. 'Both of you, come in.' After being inside, they ordered us to sit and listen.

My brother, may he rest in peace, was also an heir to our parents' fortune, 'may they rest in glory.' He never wanted to use a single cent as if punishing himself for lacking the courage to reclaim his Medical degree, which was arbitrarily revoked about two months before he passed away. He called me and said the following, and I'll tell you verbatim: 'Bill, I want you to do me a favor. You know I haven't touched a single penny of our parents' inheritance. Of course, it's my fault. But what I'm going to ask of you is, I want you to swear that you'll fulfill it.' So, I swore by God. He asked me to help the young man living with him, someone deserving of a benefit for the beautiful time he lived since the day he met you. Additionally, he mentioned that you come from a good family since he studied your family tree. So, what I'm doing is fulfilling my brother's wish, and no one has the right to object to me fulfilling his wishes. Now, I want both of you to behave like adults and stop the back and forth. You may leave, and Alexis, remember what I told you, don't disappoint me.' 'Of course not, Mr. Bill. Goodbye and see you soon.'"

"If Doris was red at the beginning of the altercation, when she left her father's study, she was purple. Despite that, she reluctantly said, 'Take care, Alexis. Goodbye.' I replied, 'Goodbye, Doris,' and I went back home to continue with my routine, which was what I enjoyed the most: studying and studying. However, I found myself entertained for a few minutes, maybe a few hours, enchanted with the image of my Mythological Goddess, analyzing the reason for her behavior. Would she still remember that kiss? Did she enjoy it and want more? Perhaps she thought I hadn't returned because I had someone else or simply because there was no one to argue with. I thought I would have the opportunity to speak with her very soon, and when she was calmer, I'd try to find out why she acted that way. So, I continued my studies, which coincided with the emotional upheavals caused by different factors.

I had the idea that my inclination towards medicine was something natural and that I would discuss that aspect with Mr. Bill, as I felt it was nobler to have the opportunity to give life rather than make money. I continued learning until I fell asleep, the book resting on the table by my head. I woke up feeling chilly and unsteady, so I headed to bed to catch a bit more sleep.

The next day was spectacular, sunny, and hot. I felt like going to the beach—it was far, but not so much that I couldn't reach it. Saving up from my allowance for expenses, I managed to buy an old car that I used to attend classes. I filled it up with gas and packed my things for the trip. I set off, excited about the prospect of a few hours of relaxation and free tanning under the sun's rays. I took my time, admiring the wonders of nature, the greenery, and the blue waters that surged to the shore, transmitting waves of energy with each sway, playfully caressing the warm sands with their foamy crests."

Parked my old car and changed into my swimwear inside. I had parked beneath swaying palm trees that moved to the rhythm of the warm gusts, producing a whisper that seemed to say, 'Hello, glad you came. Enjoy what only we can see.' It was ironic that despite being so close, they couldn't take a delightful dip, but I would do it for them. So, dressed in my tiny swim trunks, I headed through the then scorching sands and dove into the cool waters, instantly relieving the heat that was weighing on me.

As I emerged from the water and looked towards the beach, I noticed a couple of beautiful girls under umbrellas, which I hadn't taken into account upon arrival. They were gazing at me intently. I didn't take them too seriously since I was a bit introverted, so I continued swimming as best as I could. When I was a kid, I had a chance to learn a bit, but I wasn't very skilled in it.

After swimming for about an hour, I thought it was time to return and focus on what mattered most to me: learning and learning. I was passionate about philosophy and psychology, yet I couldn't find a way to apply them to heal my emotional wounds. That was one reason why I was so unsociable. As I headed towards my car, I had to pass by the umbrellas where the girls were lounging in the sun, sipping some drinks.

I tried to pass by without much interaction, but one of them coquettishly called out, 'Don't run away; we won't bite. Come, have a soda; you must be thirsty after drinking saltwater.' 'No, thank you,' I said, trying to continue on my way. However, one of them got up and walked towards me, saying, 'Don't be rude; it's impolite and ungentlemanly to reject a woman.

I felt confused and reluctantly approached the young and beautiful girls, who attentively handed me a cold soda. 'Or would you prefer a beer?' asked one of them. 'No, thanks. I don't drink alcohol; it's bad for health,' I replied. One of the three said, 'Well, one a year won't hurt,' and they all laughed. It was very embarrassing for me to be in front of three beautiful and outgoing girls, and I didn't know what to say. Fortunately, they started the conversation, introduced themselves, and asked for my name. They made comments about my well-built body and inquired if I had a girlfriend or how many I had, which further confused me. Almost stuttering, I managed to say I was single and needed to go. I thanked them for the drink, and as I was about to leave, one of them, perhaps the prettiest one, handed me her card and asked me to call her. I hurriedly made my way back to my car; I wanted to put some distance between us. I had a feeling that this encounter would bring me trouble. My instinct warned me that very soon, it would complicate my life, but I couldn't understand in what way my hunch could be true."

Eventually, I arrived back at my place. After taking a shower to rid myself of the salt from the ocean, I changed clothes and prepared something to eat. I couldn't shake the mysterious and suggestive gaze of Janeth—she was the name of the loveliest of the girls, the one who had given me her card, presumably to establish some form of friendship. She was blonde, with eyes as blue as the sea, a deep and mysterious blue, unfathomable but beautiful. Her hair cascaded over her shoulders, accentuating the perfect oval of her face. Her skin was fair and smooth, a sensation I felt when she handed me the soda. Her eyelashes were long, thick, and curved. She had a petite, upturned nose with tiny nostrils, coral-red lips, and a body that seemed to embody the Goddess Venus or perhaps the personification of Helen of Troy. Her beautifully curved breasts stirred desire, her delicate waist tempted an embrace, and her well-shaped legs could arouse carnal desire in any Olympian god or a mortal like myself.

Unintentionally, Doris, who had always lingered in my mind, had shifted to an involuntary oblivion. She disappeared as if by magic, and the presence of those beautiful and mysterious blue eyes took her place. It was surprising how someone I had barely met had managed to erase the memory of someone who had occupied my mind for so long. That face, once my adored image, had vanished, and I no longer felt that restlessness to see her. Now, a different image would accompany me—a vision that gave hope to my soul and dreams and aspirations to my young mind, still clinging to childhood dreams that refused to fade.

I read for a couple of hours, but those beautiful blue eyes remained fixed on the pages of the book I was reading. They didn't let me concentrate, but they delighted me and sparked my imagination. This led me to set aside the book and indulge in my immature adult fantasies, to dream as I did when I was a child—of the princess with blue eyes, and I her prince, whisking her away to my castle for a happily ever after. With all these dreams and illusions piling up, I retired to bed, her face lingering in my thoughts as I galloped through the valleys of sleep, in the realms of Morpheus, knowing that Eros had struck one of his arrows right into my heart.

Morning came, and I had to stop dreaming to return to reality. The first thing that came to mind was the memory of such a muse—the one that would give my mind the illusion to turn my routine into one of the most beautiful poems, to make my life the most poetic of prose, and excitedly breathe in the memory of her delightful aroma that intoxicated my thoughts at every moment. I couldn't coordinate my plans to start the day, but I knew that whatever I did, it would be great because of Janeth's presence in my thoughts. I knew that the only sensible thing to do would be to call her promptly and begin to enjoy her company day by day. So, searching for her card, I set out to call her, crossing my fingers, hoping she'd be the one to answer the phone on the other end of the line.

I was fortunate to hear her pleasant voice on the other end. "Hello," she said. "Who's calling?" "It's me, the guy from the beach. You might not remember me anymore, but I haven't stopped thinking about you." "Oh, how are you? And by the way, what's your name? Yesterday, I couldn't understand anything because everyone was speaking at once, plus the noise of the waves. But please tell me your name once more, and I promise I won't forget it this time." "Alexis," I said, "but I didn't forget yours, Janeth… nor the blue of your beautiful eyes, nor how beautiful you are overall. I'd like to invite you for a soda or something… I don't know what, but what I'd really love is for us to chat somewhere, preferably today."

Well, it seems like you're a bit hasty, but I like decisive people… they're the ones who usually succeed. Let me think about it to arrange my schedule, and call me in a couple of hours." I had been waiting anxiously for the last two hours, doing nothing but watching the clock's hands slowly move from one hour to the next. As soon as they coincided at the two-hour mark, I hurried to call. I self-justified my action, as I had never had the chance to make a date. My hands were sweating, my heart felt like it wanted to leap out of my chest, my throat was dry, and I felt an intense thirst. Unconsciously, I was holding the phone tightly, as if I feared it might slip from my grasp. Finally, I heard her voice again. "Alright, Alexis, I'll see you after classes at the café in front of the school library. Take note of the address, and we'll meet at seven, okay?" "Yes," I replied, "I'll be there.

"After ending the call, I realized I was trembling like a leaf in the wind, sweating as if I'd just run a ten-mile marathon. Maybe if I'd looked in the mirror, I would have seen the face of joy, a reflection of what I was feeling after securing a date with Janeth. I started dancing wildly, perhaps hoping to stop trembling from stress and excitement. It was my first date, and I wanted it to be memorable. So, I began thinking about what to wear and tried to calm down while waiting for the hour. I aimed to arrive on time to set a precedent for punctuality.

I needed to study some topics, but I had no desire whatsoever to do so. My focus was on Janeth, and she came first. I hoped for reciprocity. An hour before the date, I dressed in my best attire, hoping to make a good impression. It was better to wait to be expected, which would give me more minutes to enjoy by her side. I sat for about half an hour, never taking my eyes off the door, hoping to see her precious image that I had engraved in my mind. I felt the blood rush to my temples when I saw her arrive with one of her friends. It didn't matter who she came with; what mattered was that she arrived.

I stood up very gallantly as they approached and politely greeted them, asking them to sit. 'Did I keep you waiting for long?' she asked, while introducing her friend Tania, who discreetly left, making it an opportunity for us to be alone and start our dialogue after sitting down. I knew I had to let her know that I was feeling something special for her, and the first step was to find out if she had a boyfriend. It was most likely she did, as such an exceptional woman would have many admirers, and surely, one or more might have been lucky. Nevertheless, I had to ask the traditional question, but I hoped with all my soul that she'd say there was no one in her life, giving me the chance to prove my feelings for her, despite having met her just a few hours ago.

Do you have a boyfriend?" I asked, a bit flustered. "I wouldn't want to cause you any trouble." She replied somewhat annoyed, "Do you think if I had one, I would have accepted a date with you?" "I'm sorry," I said, "I'm a bit immature when it comes to matters of the heart, and I wanted to be sure so I could tell you what I'm feeling. Do you believe in love at first sight?" "Of course," she said, "that's why I agreed to see you, as I feel something similar. But I don't want to make a mistake, and I'd like to know more about you, as you appeared in my life just a few hours ago. Do you think we could get to know each other better?" "Certainly. You know," I continued, "you'll be the first woman in my life, and I'd like you to be the only one, forever. I'm an idealist; my favorite subject is Philosophy, and I'm sure you meet all the requirements to be a perfect partner. But, of course, that will have its stages, and we'll go with the flow. What do you think?"

How old are you, Alexis?" she asked, "because I don't know whether to believe you or laugh at what you're telling me. At your age, any man has at least one story to tell of their adventures." A bit embarrassed, I replied, "The life of an upright man shouldn't be a reason for laughter, and what I'm telling you is true. I shared it with you so you could form an idea of who I am and the sincerity of my intentions... I'm almost twenty." She could tell I was upset and took my hands placed on the table, saying, "Please don't be upset. It was just a silly comment; it wasn't my intention to upset you. Please forgive me." "I have nothing to forgive; for me, it's all forgotten," I said. We continued exchanging information, and I learned she was two years older than me, but I liked her very much regardless.

We ordered two sodas out of formality, as most of the time, we spent it gazing into each other's eyes, like mesmerized rabbits... under the magic of love. We went out to the café's parking lot and talked about the topics that related most to us, mainly focusing on our mutual affection and the possibilities we had ahead.

Chapter IV

For a couple of weeks, we'd been seeing each other almost every day, so we were supposedly already a couple. We kissed and talked about many things that lovers usually discuss. What I liked the most was the delicate and passionate way she kissed me, which caused me to get so excited that my underwear got wet – something I found unpleasant. Hence, one of those afternoons when we met, I asked her to come to my apartment, which had been renovated and was a very cozy place. She agreed, probably thinking it was time for our relationship to move to another level. We both arrived separately in our own means of transport and went inside. The place had a decent bed, bedside tables, and a partition separating the bedroom from the living room and the small kitchen. It also had a bathroom that had been remodeled with the latest details. My bookshelf held various scientific topics, a small CD player, and a couple of imitation paintings—a self-portrait by Van Gogh and The Last Supper by Da Vinci. Everything was tidy and painted discreetly, so her first impression was favorable, and she praised my personal touch since no one helped me with organizing it.

She became curious and checked the titles of the works. We had something in common since she had read a few titles of my books and got interested in a couple more. So, I offered to lend her the ones she wanted to read. After satisfying her curiosity and offering her something to drink, we moved on to what made us ecstatic: the most delicious kisses. I never imagined that kisses could have a flavor, but they actually gave the sensation of fruit glucose. It might have been my imagination causing me to feel sugars in those sweet kisses, but what was certain was that I felt like I was savoring the nectar of a delicate flower. Despite my age and being circumcised, I hadn't had any sexual relationships, so this was going to be my first sexual experience. She seemed more liberal and experienced in the matter, but her experience was also limited, and she felt inhibited being naked in front of me. She asked me to turn off the lights, although I left on a small lamp to appreciate, even in dim light, the beauty she possessed.

She wasn't a bad comparison to Venus, except this woman had both arms, was flesh and blood, and had other qualities, such as her beautiful blue eyes and the softness of her velvety abdomen. It was a passionate exchange between both of us. We were highly excited and couldn't wait any longer. So, she patiently waited for me to penetrate her with the delicacy that such a delicate moment deserved. It might have seemed like I was an expert lover, but the truth was, I was just learning. All I had in mind was that the first time is something that remains etched in the mind. Therefore, I aimed for it to be something unforgettable for both of us.

What delicious sensations, what a marvelous experience! I never thought something could be so thrilling, like electric charges during each of the orgasms that happened throughout the night. That feeling of euphoria we experienced when reaching the climax of each of our delightful releases, leaving us both exhausted afterward, our hearts overflowing, breaths interrupted, hands sweaty, foreheads beaded with droplets of sweat, our eyes shining not only with lust and passion but also with immense satisfaction. That day marked the culmination of the exchange of two souls that overflowed, not just with sex but also with immense love that was in full bloom.

It was the beginning of a series of daily encounters where we melded like an alloy of precious metals, merging not only our bodies but also our souls, each needing the other. We spent about three months in this beautiful state where I had just entered the wonderful world of love and had successfully passed my exam in the arts of love. Fortunately for me, love and intimacy had merged. However, I had to return to reality and continue my journey of intellectual growth, striving to become someone with a future who could offer a home and financial stability to the woman of my dreams.

I proposed to Janeth that we dedicate ourselves to finishing our studies and limit our encounters to weekends to face life's challenges with a profession. She looked at me and said, 'I don't need to work or study to have whatever I want. I'm an only child, so I can get whatever I need just by asking. We can start a business or if you want, you can work for my father in one of his businesses and have more time available to attend to me as always. How does that sound?' Truthfully, I didn't like the idea of becoming a parasite, so I asked her to at least accept my decision to finish my studies since it was very important to me.

She disagreed with my decision and threatened in her fit of anger that we would be done if I insisted on my purpose. I realized her instability hearing her threat, but I didn't let myself be intimidated and responded firmly: 'Don't behave like a spoiled child. You know very well that we can do things properly, study, and love each other while making the most of our time and achieving a good intellectual level. Otherwise, we'll be a couple of donkeys loaded with money, in case your dad likes that idea.

I reluctantly accepted my proposal, so we started studying in our next school cycle, she on her side and me on mine. But every day, she came to my little apartment to at least have a bit of sexual action, although she complained that it was very little and that maybe she had been wrong to think that I loved her. I was very focused on what I wanted, so I didn't take her comments personally. On the contrary, I made my best effort to motivate her and provide, maybe less sex, but of better quality. But I felt that little by little, she was starting to distance herself from me and lose the flame of love she professed for me, while my subconscious warned me that something bad was about to happen.

One of those nights, she arrived much later than usual and with a hint of alcohol on her breath. She looked at me and said sarcastically, 'This is what you wanted, to push me to do what I didn't want to do, but it's your fault and yours alone. But no matter what I do, I assure you that I still love you, and this is nothing more than the medicine to cure the evil of your indifference.' She began to sob, and it touched my heart. So, lovingly, I drew her close to me, holding her hands, and kissed her tenderly. I lifted her in my strong arms to take her to bed, thinking she was asking for a bit of what she demanded. So, I began to caress her and undress her slowly. When she was naked, I slid my hand between her legs and as I tried to pass my middle finger over her clitoris... I felt something viscous. Instinctively, I also felt disgust, thinking that I was touching something that someone else had left in what I thought was only mine. That delight I believed was made only for me, that pristine part of her body, had turned into something that disgusted me, something I couldn't conceive could have been stained by who knows who. Instinctively, I moved away from her side, looking at her with the greatest expression of disdain, anger, and impotence, unable to do anything to remedy the irreparable.

I asked her to leave; I couldn't wrap my head around that situation, and she couldn't make me understand that it was a mistake on her part. She claimed she regretted her actions, yet there was no justification whatsoever. Now I realized there was no perfect woman; they all, at some point, succumbed to instincts, pressures, or emotional conflicts. All the charm and magic of love disappeared in a matter of minutes. I was angry with myself for not exercising caution and giving my love entirely, without reservation or measure. Now, I realized it might be better if a woman were one-eyed, lame, or even insane, just to be certain of her fidelity, to know that there wouldn't be many desiring her. But alas, I tried to gather strength from weakness and accepted the idea that she, the one who acted wrongly, would carry the sin and consequently the penance... crime and punishment.

She left, head down and tearful, staggering—uncertain whether due to liquor or the uncertainty of her actions. Perhaps she thought it was over between us, seeing herself as a broken doll, for whom I wouldn't even give a dollar, let alone a loving glance. She didn't look back, got into her car, and drove off, her gaze blank, looking without seeing, driving like a machine. I only prayed for her soul, hoping she would find solace in reflection and heal her soul from the wounds she inflicted herself. I also prayed that she would reach home safe and sound, as often we act without thinking, when it should be just the opposite.

It had been a devastating blow for me. I no longer had the desire to continue studying, nor did I want to think about her. It wasn't worth dedicating time to someone who didn't deserve it. On the contrary, I wanted to sleep, to escape from thinking about the same thing, to avoid dwelling on the fact that my love had been tainted, to erase the memory of the beautiful woman who had occupied my soul and whom I would try to forget by any means necessary. But it was difficult to forget. How could I forget that first surrender? Those initial moments of our relationship when my hands delicately traversed her fragrant body? How could I forget the softness of her skin, the delicacy of her abdomen, and the warmth and tenderness of her feminine essence?

And so, thinking of all the beauty in our relationship, I drifted off to sleep, hoping to dream what I visualized when awake. The night passed, and upon waking, her image was the first thing that came to my mind, reviving the sadness, frustration, resentment, and desire for revenge. The idea of making her pay for what she had done crossed my mind, but my common sense reminded me: "Don't rush into thoughts of revenge. Don't stoop to her level. Instead, live your life and enjoy the good things it brings you. Time heals all wounds, and soon you'll meet someone who will help you forget. On the other hand, she will always carry the burden of guilt, which won't let her live in peace, and that will be her worst punishment."

Days after the incident, Janeth began passing by my apartment during the hours she knew I would be studying, perhaps hoping for an encounter that could lead to reconciliation. However, I had started trying to alleviate my sadness by visiting Mr. Bill's house, finding comfort in seeing Doris and fooling myself into believing that I was truly in love with her, and that the past was merely a passing phase. But the cure was worse than the ailment. Doris continued with her arrogant and incomprehensible attitude, leaving me bewildered and running away. One night, when I had already gone to bed and was listening to the radio, I heard a soft knock on the door. Though surprised, I got up to see who it was and what they wanted. As I opened the door ajar, I noticed it was Janeth. Instinctively, a morbid curiosity took hold of my mind, and I opened the door completely. Yet, at the same time, resentment shook my core. I managed to control myself and asked her to leave, explaining that our relationship was over, and there was no reason to continue something that had no reason to exist. She pleaded with me to listen to her, promising it would be the last time she asked for anything and hoping it might secure my forgiveness, even if it was the last thing I granted her.

I let her go, anyway I didn't think I would be so weak as to forgive such an offense. On the contrary, it would be an opportunity to make her feel miserable, to rub her infidelity, her lack of integrity, and the baseness of her act in her face, to show her that she was the one who had lost, and that I, thankfully, had someone else to take her place, even if that wasn't the truth. Anyway, I felt entitled to humiliate her, to put her in the place I wanted, although deep down in my soul, what I really wanted to tell her was that I still loved her and wanted her back by my side to fill my empty soul with love, to give me the sweetness of her body, her mouth, and every part of her snowy skin, to satisfy my yearning to love her and be loved. But my foolish pride, arrogance, and conceit had the upper hand, my lack of humility and my machismo... that was just who I was, and it couldn't be any other way.

I had been drinking liquor, but this time, she said to me, 'I just got drunk, but I wasn't unfaithful to you. I've learned my lesson well and I apologize for what happened before, but I want you to know that I did it for sex only, but I haven't seen that person again. It was a night of drinking, I didn't know what I was doing.' I was furious, but still looked at her compassionately, thinking that she was the way she was because she didn't have someone to guide her, she didn't have an authoritative figure to show her the right path, or because she had been given too much freedom without guidance. She looked at me pleadingly and said again, 'I want to give myself to you once more, but I'll take a bath to come back clean and repentant. May I?'

I let her go to the bathroom; I wanted her to take a shower to clear her head and be able to return home. I didn't want anything else but for her to arrive safe and sound. My desire for her was well under control, and the last thing I wanted was to have sex with someone I considered impure and unworthy due to her betrayal.

So, she went to the bathroom and turned on the taps to fill the bathtub; she wanted a foamy shower. She knew where I kept the foaming soap; she emptied it and started shaking it while undressing. I couldn't help but look at her beautiful and delicious body, which despite the betrayal and everything else, hadn't lost its charm. And so, watching her and hearing her say incoherent things, she got into the foam and started playing with it, inviting me to join the game.

When you told me, 'Now I'm all clean, as you like,' or do you prefer that I go find someone to take your place? Or are you just playing hard to feel like a domineering macho? Come, I'll ease your anger by behaving like a good girl and fulfilling all your whims.' I felt the urge to cover her mouth, to stop her from speaking those hurtful words that worsened the wound in my soul. 'Do you want to kill me, don't you? So you won't have to desire me without feeling guilty, or to hide your weakness in wanting me as you do. Come on, don't be a coward, take me and forget that I've been with another man, even though the truth is, I've been with others before you, so what difference does one more make? I'm not your property anyway. Coward, come!' She shouted, and I couldn't contain myself; I pushed her head into the bathtub, where she stopped uttering a word. After a few seconds, I let her go for her to breathe again, but as she lifted her head, she continued with her string of offensive comments that made me lose my composure. Still, I tried to walk away to the living room, but she said, 'Run away, coward, that's all you can do instead of facing reality and forgiving me or killing me once and for all, so I don't feel like a common prostitute, making my heart bleed just as you say yours does.'

Come and look at me. Do you think you're better than me just because you haven't deceived me? Or do you think only you can make me happy? And do you doubt that someone else could have made me happier than you?' I couldn't bear to hear another word. I knew she was drunk, but that didn't give her the right to keep insulting my manly dignity. So, I grabbed her by the head and submerged her again in the bathtub. This time, I intended to keep her underwater for longer, so she would finally shut up, leave me alone, and be at peace. Allowing this to happen had been a mistake; it shouldn't have been like this. It only made me despise her more for her behavior. I kept thinking about all the things she had done to me. Also, I didn't realize the strength in my hands and didn't notice that she had started convulsing, then becoming motionless. Suddenly, I realized she had stopped moving. Instinctively, I pulled her head out of the water. She was still and made no sound. I shook her vigorously, nothing. I blew on her face, nothing. I felt fear, a lot of fear. I tried mouth-to-mouth resuscitation, but it was the same effect, no response. I took her out of the bathtub and rushed her to the bed, attempting CPR and mouth-to-mouth resuscitation, but it was futile. She had passed away.

It occurred to me to call the paramedics, but once again, I was afraid. I thought that by the time they arrived, she would be even colder than she was, and on top of that, I could be accused of at least involuntary manslaughter. My entire future would have gone down the drain. So, trying to calm myself down, I started planning what would be most appropriate in that situation. I felt anguish, guilt, and anger for not thinking about the consequences of letting her in and not reciprocating what she said. Why didn't I give her some sex and then let her sleep? Even if the next day I would have told her it was over when she was sober. Well, I had no way to bring her back to life, but I had to find a way to get rid of her body in a manner that left no loose ends.

I peeked out the door to check for witnesses. There was no illuminated window, and it was an area with very few houses and minimal lighting due to the trees in the yard, along with the trees the city had planted on the edge of the street. Her car was parked in front of my house, so I came up with a plan that could work if it played out as I had planned. I dressed her after drying her with a towel, put on her shoes, and took her bag. She was still soft, and holding her by the waist, we began walking toward her car. I deactivated the alarm, opened the passenger side door, carefully placed her inside, making sure to fasten her seatbelt. I started the car and headed towards the beach, where I would initiate phase two of my sinister plan.

If things are not done correctly, they tend to get more and more complicated, and this was no exception. Now, I was becoming a criminal with aggravating circumstances by covering up my involuntary manslaughter, trying to erase evidence, and dispose of the body of a beautiful and young woman. But my regret went further as I thought about the pain it would cause her family, the anguish her parents would feel knowing that their only daughter would no longer bring them the joy of her presence. Perhaps from her comments or whims, or for whatever reason, I thought it would be an irreparable loss.

We reached the most secluded spot on the beach, and I parked after driving the car a couple of blocks with the lights off. I took her out in the same tender way I had placed her in the car. We walked embraced until we reached where the waves met the sandy shore. I had brought a towel and laid it on the sand, placing Janeth's bag on it. Then, I undressed her until she was only in her bra and bikini. I had been careful not to leave any kind of fingerprints on the steering wheel and the parts I touched. I also cleaned the keychain and the car's ignition key. I held Janeth against one of my legs while crouched down arranging things. Then, I took her in my arms and waded into the tepid waters of the sea. I gave her a tender kiss and, with tears in my eyes, released her into the water where she began to float, like a twig swayed by the force of the waves' movements.

And I left without even looking back. I felt immense remorse; she had been the first and greatest love of my life. With her, I knew what it was to love and have sex, I had tasted the flavor of kisses. I didn't know if I could ever love again or if the memory of what happened would prevent me from being a normal man again. There were many conjectures crowding my mind, many moments of tension experienced in just a few hours. I walked for an incalculable amount of time, and at dawn, I reached my house and collapsed onto the bed like a sack of potatoes. I didn't even have the strength to take off my shoes and fell asleep. Perhaps out of exhaustion, or because my brain was unable to answer all the questions posed and chose to shift into the subconscious state.

I woke up at ten in the morning, unusual for me, but I believed there was a justified reason. I got up and headed to the bathroom. I was afraid to enter, but knowing it was daytime, I tried to think of something else. It was a quick shower, and when I looked at myself in the mirror to shave, I felt her sea-blue eyes focusing on mine, accusing me of what I had done. 'It was an accident,' I muttered, all disheveled. 'Yes, an accident.' I had to wait a few minutes to finish shaving. I didn't know what to do, but I still had to go to classes to avoid arousing any suspicion. I had to continue leading an apparently normal life and do what I always did. I had a great power of concentration, so I knew I could manage it.

I had a good alibi because I couldn't deny knowing her, but nobody had seen us together. Besides, due to her economic position, she always tried to avoid any suggestion that we were more than friends. Just the girl she introduced me to a few months ago, but I was sure she wouldn't even remember me. Also, I was confident that nobody had noticed the end of it all, and they would consider it an accident for her. They would find alcohol in her bloodstream and water in her lungs, presuming that while she was drunk, she decided to take a bath and drowned. It was logical, and I hoped that's what the detective investigating would think.

There was only one issue—the water in her lungs was sweet and had traces of soap. But then, how would they know where she died? I knew forensic sciences were highly advanced, but it was a very difficult situation to trace. Additionally, they would find traces of DNA from the man she had been with just a few days ago, or who knows, maybe they'd link her to someone else and not to someone as poor as me. Lastly, if I were discovered, my fate would be sealed, and I'd serve my sentence as the law dictates.

On the evening news, I realized they had found the body. They emphasized the danger of drinking and doing something irresponsible, like swimming while intoxicated and alone. They also commented that there were no suspicions of assault or robbery, suggesting it might have been a type of love-induced suicide. Deep down, I believed they were somewhat right, maybe she, deep in her soul, wanted to die rather than bear the guilt of breaking my heart and hers simultaneously. Perhaps that's why she had died so quickly, and I didn't have time to revive her, no matter how much effort I put in. Well, any excuse was good enough to alleviate the weight of the sorrow I felt in my soul, especially given the immense love I felt for her.

Anyway, I got rid of all the sand embedded in my clothes and shoes. I was lucky that a strong gust had probably erased the footprints I left on the beach in the early hours. Now, I just had to stick to my story that I had spent the night alone, studying as usual. I knew her, but only superficially, and hadn't seen her for a few days. In the morning, I turned on the small TV again to watch the news, and they reported that an autopsy had been ordered to determine the cause of her death but that they didn't have any suspects in sight. I felt immense relief, and my anxiety gradually lessened. It was disturbing to be in the place where her death had occurred; I felt her presence was noticeable throughout the tiny apartment and tried to spend most of my time outside.

I started to consider the idea of moving out, but it was too early to do so without arousing suspicions from those who knew me and had seen me in her company on occasions, even if it was just talking since our relationship was kept secret due to social reasons. So, I had no choice but to get used to the idea of living with her presence in my mind, feeling observed while in the apartment. When I was on the street or at school, my tasks kept me away from memories of her and the unfortunate events.

Six weeks after the incident, I went to visit Mr. Bill and suggested that I wanted to change my address. I explained that I was about to finish school and would soon attend university. I proposed that he authorize me to travel to Miami, where I could continue my education at the next level. He was very pleased with my achievements and fulfilling his late brother's wishes. Being a businessman, he considered it an investment since he mentioned I could provide legal services for his business interests in general. We agreed that after finishing my exams, I could leave to search for housing and apply for admission to the Law School. Although I was inclined towards Medicine, I couldn't contradict him. It was important to me that he was content, making it enjoyable to sponsor me.

After finishing the exams, I had a final conversation with him before departing for a place with more challenges due to its larger population. However, I had faced worse when I was just a child, so I knew I could handle whatever came my way. When I arrived at Mr. Bill's house, I encountered Doris, the haughty and arrogant one, the one who perhaps deserved to be in Janeth's place (I thought), but then I regretted it because no one has the right to wish upon others what they wouldn't want for themselves. After a brief hello, I continued on my way to meet with Mr. Bill. He treated me like his son and said, 'Look, young man, the first thing is to focus on your studies and nothing else. Stay away from people who could be a bad influence and avoid getting involved with girls. After becoming a professional, you'll have all the time and money in the world to have as many as you want. I'll give you a check for rent, deposit, etc. Also, money for the hotel and food while you find a place to live. I'll also give you some for the university enrollment, and if it's not enough, just call me to solve the problem. I wish you the best of luck and keep me informed of any detail, no matter how small it may seem.

He wrote the checks and handed them to me. With the other hand, he gave me a firm handshake and a pat on my shoulder, saying, 'Finally, best of luck.' I left his office/study and headed towards the street. At the exit door, there was Doris, with her impregnable expression, that look of indifference, and a bitter expression on her lips. I couldn't understand how such a jovial girl had transformed into such an unpleasant person. Despite my attempts to get closer, that charismatic and joyful girl was unrecognizable and seemed unwilling to change. But surely she wanted to tell me something, and that was why she was standing there waiting for me to leave. So, as I reached where she was standing, I had no choice but to bid her goodbye. However, instead of responding to my farewell, she reproached me.

You're leaving without saying goodbye, right? If I hadn't waited for you here, I wouldn't know when and where you would have left. And mind you, you're still nobody. I can imagine the day you become a lawyer, that is, if you ever graduate. Anyway, I wish you luck, and don't forget to keep my father informed because he cares more about you than about me.' Now, I understood the reason for her bitterness. Perhaps she felt jealous of her father's attention. It occurred to me that I would do something to dispel that idea from her mind. So, I said, 'It's not as you imagine. He's just trying to fulfill his brother's last wish (may he rest in peace). As far as you're concerned, you're his everything. He only thinks about your happiness and wants to see you married one day, giving him grandchildren before he leaves this world, as is normal. He hasn't spent a single cent of his fortune. The money he gives me for my expenses is solely from Don Daniel's inheritance, your uncle. He also left me a bank account, but I don't want to touch a single dollar until I have the opportunity to set up my law firm or medical practice. I'm very interested in studying Medicine rather than Law.'

Well, I'm leaving, and don't forget what I told you. I'll have time to talk to your father about my academic concerns. Take care and regain that happiness you possessed when I first met you. Remember that you're still an important part of my life, and maybe when I become a professional, if I manage to do so, then I'll have something different to offer you, and that will be when we'll talk again.' After extending my hand to say goodbye, she pulled me towards her, giving me a tight hug and a kiss on the cheek. She said, 'Don't forget to think about me, even occasionally, and if you can, send me a few lines from time to time.

Chapter V

I arrived in Miami, feeling like a fish out of water. It was vastly different from the peace I had experienced for so many years, but nevertheless, it was a very beautiful place. People were very sociable and warm-hearted. I stayed at a small but lovely and clean hotel. The next morning, I bought a newspaper to look for available apartments near the university. At the same time, I went to the university to fill out my admission application. I was very excited, and little by little, I had started to forget what happened with Janeth. I still felt guilty, but I could live with it. In the end, as if seeking solace, I accepted that it had been just an accident. Moreover, I wanted to start a new chapter in my life, so I began by focusing on life's purpose: to improve oneself and enjoy it to the fullest."

"I found myself browsing through the Miami Herald, looking through its classifieds in hopes of finding something affordable to live in. Tuition was going to be costly, especially for fields like Law or Medicine, both of which interested me, although I leaned towards Medicine. After filling out my application to UM, I planned to head to one of the residential complexes I had found in the newspaper. They had simple apartments that suited my needs and what I could afford.

I closed the deal on the apartment within the first twenty-four hours of my arrival in Miami. Now, I just had to wait for the entrance exams. But before that, I wanted to talk to Mr. Bill about my concern regarding the Medicine career. I hoped he would understand and agree. I didn't want to upset him; he was someone I highly respected. After trying to call his house with no answer, I dialed his office, and his secretary answered. After explaining who I was, I managed to speak to him. After asking about his and Doris's well-being, I moved on to the reason for my call and shared my concerns. 'Young man,' he said, 'I know you have talent for any career, but I suggest you study Law. It's a field that can make you wealthy quickly, and there are job opportunities with me. Besides, it won't enslave you like Medicine. It's admirable to want to help others and heal the world, but it's even more admirable to look after your own interests. There will be others to fill the gap in Medicine, and you'll take your place in my business.

Alright," I said, "I'll do as you say. I'll become a lawyer... count on it. Have a good day, and I'll soon be sending you the acceptance papers for the Law School, as per your wish and vision. Please give my regards to Doris." I had a few days before classes started, so I headed to the beach to take a good dip. Although I didn't intend to be noticed by girls, I didn't go unnoticed by many of them. I think it was because of my muscular body and good-looking face, so I sometimes felt as if I was being pursued by so many gazes. I wasn't narcissistic at all; in fact, I always tried to appear less appealing by wearing slightly larger clothes than my natural size. Still, I was the center of attention for the female gender, especially. There was always a man or two looking at me challengingly, almost as if in competition.

While my commitment was to study Law, I enrolled in two Medicine courses. It was something that attracted me like a bee to honey, and with nothing else to do, I knew I could manage them. I would study during the supposed rest time, considering they could help relieve the stress from the other courses. Anatomy and Biology were among my passions, and I was sure I'd grasp them well. I was interested in Psychology and Philosophy, knowing they would have a direct relationship with my career in some way. I'd probably read additional treatises to quench my thirst for knowledge along the way.

"Pleasure enveloped me as I reveled in the beautiful beaches of Miami. Everything was so beautiful, filled with sunshine and beautiful women everywhere. However, I felt this sense of guilt that prevented me from considering a relationship that could fill my soul with emotional connections. I was haunted by trauma, afraid that I might lose control of my emotions and harm another innocent person. So, I became evasive and solitary, naturally excelling as a student, earning top grades, which made me the center of attention for the opposite sex. I would lock myself in my apartment for two consecutive days, typically on weekends. While most students went out partying, I focused on studying my two extra courses and catching up on other subjects.

I had been in the same routine for two months, so focused on it that I didn't realize one of my study partners had been observing me. She knew where I lived and what I did in my spare time outside of classes. One Sunday, after reading for a few hours, I stepped out of my apartment door to clear my head. My vision was slightly blurry, and I wanted to regain clarity to continue my focus. As I looked across the street, I noticed a beautiful girl, a classmate, standing next to a sports car. Initially, I thought it was a coincidence, but as I tried to go back into my apartment, she caught my attention by waving at me. At first, I thought she was just saying hello, but when I returned the greeting, she signaled for me to wait for her.

I had no choice, so she approached me with light steps. As she got closer, she greeted me with a lot of excitement and said, "Hi, I'm Diana. I didn't know you lived here. I'm waiting for a friend, but it seems like she's running late (she lied), and maybe she won't come anymore... Would you invite me in?" I had no choice but to ask her in, feeling a bit embarrassed about the mess in my apartment. "Please excuse the mess; I've been very busy and haven't had much time to tidy up." "No worries, I understand. The reason is that you dedicate more time to studying than to a trivial thing like tidying up. But if you want, I can help you," she said. "No worries, I'll do it later. Would you like a soda or juice? I don't have anything else; I don't promote alcohol since it's harmful to health," I said.

I'll have juice, and I like your way. Now I understand why you're successful in your studies. You're tenacious when it comes to learning. That's why men envy you, and women adore you. You're the man any woman would want as her boyfriend or preferably as her husband," she said. "Do you think you could satisfy a woman's curiosity? Tell me what it is; I can't say yes without knowing the question," I said. She asked, "Are you married? Do you have a girlfriend? If you're not married, it seems like you are." "I'll answer if you promise not to spread it around. Deal?" "Sure," she replied excitedly. "I promise," she assured me. "I'm single and not in any romantic commitment. I'm not seeking one either, as I want to do well in the career I'm studying."

She seemed disappointed but tried to hide it and said, "At least until you find a woman who shares the same aspirations as you, someone who'll reignite the love you have with the extinguished flame. But with the warmth of another love, it will surely reignite, have you thought about it?" She was a very beautiful girl, perhaps in her early twenties. Her stunning caramel-colored eyes radiated passion, surrounded by long eyelashes and well-defined eyebrows. Her petite, straight nose and a constant smile on her thick, red, and fleshy lips that invited a kiss. All framed within a perfectly oval face. She stood at about 5'9", and her figure did justice to her name, Diana... like Diana the huntress, the Goddess of Olympus. Her fair, almost white skin contrasted with a slender waist, wide hips, shapely buttocks, and a bust that would make any Amazonian warrior envious.

However, I couldn't lose my composure and fall into what might be a game or a bet between schoolgirls, or who knows, anything was possible. Besides, I still carried the sorrow of what happened and the memory of the indomitable Doris, who haunted my thoughts. Sometimes, I felt her so close, but in reality, she was as far away as the other side of the Milky Way. I stopped the flattery and asked not to talk about that subject for the time being. I had a promise to keep, and if I ever had a girlfriend, it had to be a secret as my mentor shouldn't know. That would be the condition for my hypothetical relationship.

You're right to be who you are," she said. "You deserve a girl who has many attributes, not someone plain like me." "Don't say that. You know you're beautiful. But we're not discussing your beauty or your love, as we've only known each other for a few days or weeks. Wouldn't you prefer to talk about any topic related to our studies instead of delving into complex themes like love?" I suggested. She responded, "Love is a philosophical matter, and philosophy is part of our major, so it's a good subject we could delve into if you agree." "I don't think it's advisable to discuss deep topics," I said. "Since you came for a visit, if you want, we can arrange a study session and discuss any topic you wish. How about that?" "Okay," she accepted. We agreed to postpone it for the following week, and she bid farewell with a handshake and a quick kiss on my cheek.

I didn't want to commit in any way; my main goal was to study and graduate with top grades. There would be time for that later, as Mr. Bill had mentioned. I believed he was right, though it was a bit challenging for a young man with my physical appearance, which seemed to attract the opposite sex like a magnet. Nevertheless, I tried my best to remain serious to avoid any situation that might lead me off course. I also considered that a man should be chaste just like women since a man also has a reputation to uphold.

Ultimately, I believed I was living in a different era in a modern world. Still, I was cautious not to entirely involve my feelings. The next week, I had a chance to talk to her. She looked lovely in her two-piece red dress, a short skirt, and a pronounced neckline that heightened the allure. I tried to shift my thoughts elsewhere and quickly asked the usual, "How are you?" etc. She gave the appropriate answers, and we ran out of things to say. Sensing the unease, I tried to ask about scheduling our session to delve into a topic. I asked, "Have you chosen the day and time for our discussion? It's about the philosophy class, and I think the topic is love." "Yes, of course. When do you think would be the right day for us to meet and delve into a purely platonic topic, considering you have no interest in getting tangled up in something as beautiful as love?

"We met over the weekend, as we had agreed. She brought her treatise of Plato, and I was glad she had something to base our discussion on. I did point out that all of Plato's basic ideas were teachings from Socrates. Nevertheless, we had plenty to delve into on the topic. I suggested that love for teaching, wisdom, and beauty is where the true origin of love lies. She agreed, mentioning that Plato was seeking the perfect society, promoting equal rights, especially for learning. She also added that physical love was a desire for immortality and eternity, a need to perpetuate the species and an ego to satisfy oneself with beauty by eternalizing generations. We concluded that love can be platonic when it's pure and doesn't require the physical relationship with the other person. There was no need for us to question to know our knowledge or our ignorance; we were filling our virtue with knowledge and didn't have the vice of ignorance.

We continued discussing other topics of academic interest until hunger told us it was time for a break and some food to ease it. So, we ordered pizza and ate. Then, I invited her to watch any movie on TV to clear our minds from so much learning. It was then, observing her closely, that I noticed her many attributes and qualities. She had a very cultured and graceful way of eating and drinking, and her way of walking and her gestures were quite refined. I could also take a closer look at the beauty of her form and the provocativeness of her movements. Instinctively, I asked her if she was afraid of being alone in the company of a man. She replied: 'If you were just any man, maybe. But knowing that besides being a man, you are also a true gentleman, I wouldn't worry at all.' All I could say was: 'I appreciate the compliment.'

We continued developing various topics in which we always agreed and reasoned in the best way possible. As the night fell, I had to ask if it was getting late for her. She replied: 'Don't worry, I have no one waiting for me. Remember, I live on the University campus, and my roommate doesn't interfere in my affairs, just as I don't interfere in hers, except if she needs advice or help of any kind. Plus, I don't think you would deny me a spot to sleep if it gets too late, right?'

I felt a bit embarrassed, unsure of what to say. My initial reaction was to offer her my bed, suggesting I could sleep on the sofa if needed. "Don't worry, I'll only stay for a while longer and then leave, but if you ask me... I'd gladly keep you company," she responded. I added, "Anyway, tomorrow is Sunday, no need to worry, so we can take our time. If you'd like, we could stop studying and really enjoy the night—watch a movie, have some pastries and a drink. What do you say? You can either leave afterwards or stay for company, and I'll promise to behave. I trust you, but I'm not sure if I can behave myself with a man like you around." I sensed her intense and provocative gaze, seeing in her eyes the fiery desires of animal instinct. She seemed eager to devour the man standing before her, unhesitant to behave in the most seductive manner possible. I was playing hard to get, but deep down, I also yearned for the same. I wanted to indulge and be indulged, to experience a whirlwind of passion that would make me forget the things that troubled me and made me forget the wonders of love and being loved, owning and being possessed, transporting us to a different world through love and sex.

I wanted to forget the unfortunate incident I had been involved in, hoping to shake off that dreadful experience that lingered in my mind. Now, an opportunity arose to start a new chapter in my romantic life, and she was a woman who fulfilled every expectation of any man. So, I began to let things unfold as they should, allowing her to use all her persuasion to seduce me, even though it was my decision at that precise moment. She unbuttoned her neckline a bit, letting her breasts be visible as if they were attacking me. Her gaze turned intense, with malice and suggestion. Her breathing became heavy, and her body emitted pheromones that stirred my animal instincts, making me more inclined towards promiscuity.

She hesitated to make a move, seemingly unsure, as if she was afraid to face a magnificent male specimen and anticipated an unforgettable, perhaps addictive, night. Still a bit trembling, she approached me, probing, "Do you find me desirable?" "Absolutely, I am so tempted to kiss you. Do you think that's possible?" It seemed those were the words she had been waiting for. Immediately, she moved closer, so our lips were just milliseconds apart. Our breaths felt so close and agitated that we couldn't contain the overwhelming desire invading us. We surrendered to a desperate kiss that we had both been longing for, seemingly for endless moments.

I didn't know if all mouths had the same taste, but the truth was that I felt like I was drinking the honey from a beautiful flower. I felt that their saliva was the nectar of the gods, that the effect that this delicious nectar was having on me was awakening the man that had been asleep for a few months due to the unfortunate event. Like magic, it made all of that fade into oblivion, giving way to an endless source of energy in my body that transformed into a reservoir of "caresses, kisses, and sex... a lot of sex, and that's how we were until the early hours of dawn, when exhaustion finally took hold of us and forced us to surrender, seeking refuge in the arms of Morpheus, who welcomed us immediately.

We woke up like Adam and Eve, completely naked. I was the first to awaken and I was ecstatic to see the beauty of her body—the fullness of her breasts with rosy nipples, the flatness of her abdomen, and the lushness of her Venus mound. Her delicate curves would have made Aphrodite envious, and the smoothness of her skin invited touch. Instinctively, I began to caress her entire body. When she opened her lovely eyes and realized her nudity, she instinctively sought something to cover herself. Immediately, I protested: 'Don't be selfish, depriving me of such a delightful sight. Please, let me see it once more.' A bit embarrassed, she removed what covered her and allowed my curious eyes to behold her marvelous body, seeming to have escaped from a work of Michelangelo.

Later, I searched for the clock on the nightstand; I wanted to know the time to fulfill our plan for a delicious breakfast. It was nine a.m.—a good time for a nutritious breakfast and a delightful cup of coffee.

True to my word, I shot up and delved into the small kitchen. I had always liked keeping my promises, and this wouldn't be an exception. I began preparing delicious eggs, a portion of bacon, and toast, while the delightful aroma of coffee permeated the room. While I was busy in the culinary domain, she had taken a refreshing bath and looked as fresh as a daisy, her seductive body semi-covered by one of my red sports shirts she found in one of my drawers, fitting her wonderfully. After serving breakfast, we sat down to eat and to gaze at each other, reminiscing about the marvelous moments we shared during our long night of passion.

We didn't want to know anything else beyond our new romance, so we devoted ourselves to loving each other, to enjoying every available moment as if the world were to vanish the next day. We loved each other passionately, though truthfully, I think it was driven by our long abstinence, our youth, and the strong attraction we felt for each other. We completely forgot about our studies. After all, what better anatomy lesson than observing the pinnacle of human beauty in her body?

Well, it was time to return to reality, and we had to say goodbye for now. I asked her not to discuss our affair; I didn't want anyone to share what was happening in my private life. I wanted no one to have access to the intimacy that only we had the right to know and enjoy. People always insist on judging things they cannot comprehend because they haven't experienced them personally. I didn't know how far our relationship could go, but I hoped to enjoy it for as long as it lasted and give my best until the very end. I bid her farewell before opening the door—I didn't want prying eyes or false witnesses. Though a bit confused, she accepted my terms and said goodbye.

After she left, I cleaned up the mess that was left behind and prepared myself for the busy week of student activities ahead. I didn't want anything to detract from my focus on my goals. I aimed for the best grades and to accumulate knowledge in my mind. I wanted to excel; it was a moral obligation in memory of my good friend and mentor, 'Daniel,' whose advice and dedication to teaching me were always in my thoughts. The painful memory of that tragic night had slowly faded away. I wanted to erase all bad memories and convince myself that it wasn't my fault. With Diana's presence, I felt I had more help. She would be the remedy to heal my soul from any guilt complex. I was confident she would be that for me. With that idea in my mind, I finished preparing for the next day, trusting it would be a day filled with emotions and new knowledge.

I didn't like the idea of her always being on my mind; I didn't want her to interfere with my academic achievements. However, her beautiful eyes kept appearing in my thoughts at every moment. A bit concerned, I went to sleep, although it was difficult to forget such delightful moments, making it hard to drift off.

It was a radiant day, filled with sunshine that flooded my body with energy, making me feel like an exceptional man, eager to embrace life to the fullest. I had a strong desire to absorb all the knowledge my young mind needed, to store it in my gray matter, in my hard drive longing to be filled with wisdom. I aimed to perform like a man capable of overcoming life's toughest obstacles. I had the resilience of a winner and would do the impossible to meet my life's expectations. I wanted to be someone special, to help those who lacked the capacity to fend off life's adversities.

I marched towards my encounter with wisdom, always eager to acquire new knowledge, especially on that day. I felt that the new relationship with Diana would bring something positive into my life. It would help me forget the past and focus on new expectations. I sensed that from that moment on, I would have someone to share both the good and not-so-good times with. I would feel appreciated and cared for by someone who made me feel important in life. She was special, had a very discreet and suggestive way of giving herself. She was beautiful, intelligent, refined, and probably from a good family. Although the idea of family didn't matter much, because if our relationship flourished, we would probably create our own... our own family.

As if waiting for me, the first thing I encountered at the educational institution was her intense and suggestive gaze. Her delicate lips formed the sign of a kiss, and I felt my skin tingle as I remembered the moments from the previous night. I felt the influence she was exerting on me and I got scared—scared that what I was starting to feel for her, this budding romance, might spiral out of control. I feared that it could turn into something that, in the future, might hurt me due to the intensity of my feelings. Something that could transform into an obsessive love, beyond all reason, and could even harm both of us.

I chose to revert to the focus I had before seeing her, and with a simple greeting, I headed to my study hall. It was very difficult to concentrate on the topics at hand, but with my power of self-persuasion, I eventually managed to return to normalcy and continue with my learning routine. At the end of the day, she was standing at the building's entrance, her expectant gaze scanning everywhere. When she spotted me, she tensed up, like a predator eyeing its prey. As she approached me with a wonderful smile, she asked me with a hint of embarrassment, 'How was your day?' I replied, 'Not very good, I missed you and your delightful caresses. And you, how was yours?' She responded, 'I would have had a better time by your side, with those caresses capable of melting an iceberg.'

We walked slowly, chatting about everything without really knowing what we were talking about. It was as if what mattered most to us was what would happen in a short while. She and I already had plans made in advance (subconsciously), as we felt that the previous night hadn't been able to satisfy our repressed instincts for a long time. It would have taken a seventy-two-hour day to satisfy our young bodies and our lustful minds. Although inexperienced in love matters, we didn't hesitate to enjoy the pleasures of sex.

'Come on, I'll drive,' she said, taking the wheel. I didn't resist; I wanted to be swept away by her lustful desire. The faster we got there, the better. I wanted the same things she did. I felt the same eagerness to possess her and be possessed by her. I wanted to savor the delicious nectar of her lips, to feel the scent of her hair, the salty taste of her sweat in the heat of our bodily battle, to transform the warmth of our bodies into a fire that would burn our souls with intense passion. All this excitement made it hard for us to think rationally; we just wanted to arrive quickly at what would be our love nest.

And we arrived. I asked her to come up to my apartment out of courtesy, though I believed it was unnecessary; she would have come up regardless, as I was sure she understood the language of my gaze. She could sense my pheromones, predisposing her to our encounter. We were like opposite poles of two magnets, mutually attracted. We climbed the few steps and reached the door. I had to find the key, but I wished I could just break the door down. Finally inside, after tossing the books onto the sofa, we stood face to face. We wanted to say something, but it was impossible. It seemed like everything we could say was already known by both of us. I felt like we were twin souls; we didn't have to say anything because we knew and understood everything about each other.

And we looked at each other, as if trying to communicate telepathically that it was time for action, the moment we had been yearning for all day, the complement to what we were feeling—this beautiful thing called love. I gently took her and drew her closer, holding her by her neck until her mouth was inches from mine. I softly touched her lips with mine, our tongues meeting. I felt the nectar of her delicious mouth invading mine, our lips merging in a delightful and vibrant kiss that made our bodies tremble and our minds wander in an ethereal space.

Gradually, clothing started to fall, and our bodies began to sense the static charge, which tingled our skin and accelerated the beat of our hearts. Our breaths became faster, and our minds grew cloudy. We began to feel the touch of our sexes devouring each other, rhythmically and without haste, savoring to the fullest a gift of life.

We were suspended in time, for when we regained enough lucidity to realize reality, it was already night. We felt hungry and had to heed the needs of our bodies. After all, we were human, with qualities and flaws. She put on my shirt, which looked like a mini-dress on her and made her look quite sexy. She headed to the kitchen to prepare something to eat, wanting to demonstrate her culinary skills, to show me that she had the qualities to be a good homemaker—because the other qualities were obviously there, and very good. We enjoyed the rest of the night, taking a break to watch a movie before diving into another session of pleasure and energy expenditure, until Morpheus welcomed us into his arms and provided us with a good rest.

Morning came again, and the routine continued. This time, she insisted on taking me to class, but I reminded her of the promise she had made—that our relationship had to go unnoticed due to different factors that were very important to me. Of course, she remembered and showed some anger towards the promise, saying, 'I wish everyone knew how much we love each other and how happy we are.' However, without a choice, she reluctantly left, stomping her feet on the floor like a spoiled child. Of course, she didn't forget to remind me that we would see each other at night, at the same place... my apartment.

I also headed to the educational center, continuously learning. My mind was like a sponge, always absorbing all kinds of knowledge. It became more and more obsessive each day, the way I was determined to gather the desired knowledge. However, as I anticipated, she had become a compulsive lover. Every day, she found a different way to entice me, interfering with my eagerness to learn from the books I brought from the school library. Whenever I noticed, she was suggestively caressing me, and we ended up in bed where I had to put all my effort into satisfying her until she fell asleep. Only then could I concentrate on my main obsession.

I thought I might be getting irrational in my way of learning and considered consulting a psychologist to know if I was acting correctly or if I had some compulsive emotional disorder. Besides my learning obsession, her obsession for seeking more pleasure had started. She had begun practicing almost ridiculous and quite masochistic positions, sometimes a bit dangerous from my analysis.

"That night, as usual, after I had arrived and prepared something for dinner, she appeared on the scene with her innocent face and angelic smile. I knew she had cooked for both of us, and after washing her hands, she sat at the table. I was truly loving her; otherwise, I don't think I would have been so accommodating or patient with her. However, I was beginning to worry about her behavior, which, though delightful, was also dangerous.

After dinner, I asked her to watch some TV as I wanted to focus on one of the subjects that would be discussed the next day. I wanted to be prepared for the dialogue. A bit annoyed, she went to the sofa and turned on the television, engrossed in a program. After a couple of hours, when I had read enough, I prepared to take a shower before going to bed, as I wanted to be attentive during the dialogue. As soon as she saw me heading to the bathroom, she jumped up as if propelled by a spring and followed me there. I couldn't resist as she started undressing and showing me her beautiful and delicious body. She joined me, caressing me with the touch of her smooth and fragrant skin.

We caressed each other under the coolness of the water, passionately kissing, causing extreme arousal. We emerged from the bath like torches, our minds confused by the desire to satisfy our instincts and extinguish the fire of passion burning within us. We headed to the bedroom and entwined in an embrace that fused our bodies, initiating a session of inexplicable sensations. She experienced her first orgasm within minutes, while I took my time. I wanted to feel the unique contractions of her sexual muscles. However, suddenly she said, 'Please, squeeze my throat... I want to feel the agony of ecstasy. They say those who die by hanging are the happiest... please do it.' I was surprised but still tried to comply, hoping to fulfill her desires the way she enjoyed the most. It was a rather 'crazy' request, but I was surprised by the contractions she caused in me. I tightened a bit more, believing that when she felt the agony of suffocation, she contracted her vaginal muscles more. But I got scared when suddenly her whole body went limp—she had passed out due to lack of oxygen to her brain. It brought to mind how my first love had died. Tremendously scared, I revived her with chest compressions and blowing air onto her face.

It was a delightful yet worrying experience. We had crossed the boundaries of normality, and now I was very concerned. Because the vast majority of things that provide us extreme pleasure become an addiction, and addictions have consequences. When we returned to normality, when the scare was over, more for me than for her since she didn't realize what had happened as she had fainted and when she came to, she didn't know how it had happened. So, I told her what had happened and begged her not to make up things that could eventually cause us different kinds of problems. She laughed it off and said, 'Didn't you like it? It's one thing to find it pleasant, another thing when it could cause death for you and a bitter sentence for me as an accomplice. Forget it,' she said, quickly kissing me the way only she knew how, and we continued loving each other, albeit without the neck grip.

"Once again, she had stayed over at my apartment, and the routine repeated itself as it did whenever she stayed. I prepared breakfast after my invigorating shower, while she did the same to be ready by the time it was served. While we were eating, I suggested that we stop seeing each other for a while, at least until the exam season was over, and she could reconsider the ideas that had recently arisen within her. This suggestion displeased her greatly and sparked a discussion. Not wanting the argument to escalate, I asked her to calm down, suggesting we discuss it again in the afternoon if she agreed. We then went our separate ways to the study center.

As I made my way, I was pondering that the relationship was going beyond the boundaries of normalcy, edging toward dangerous limits, stress in the relationship, and intransigence. She was unwilling to compromise in her pursuit of finding more pleasure in sex, and I didn't want to expose her to any accidents, fearing a tragic incident like the one that took the life of my first love. Of course, she couldn't understand, not knowing what had happened, and logically, I couldn't tell her. So, I needed to figure out an effective way to rid her mind of these aberrations that endangered our lives, no matter how we might see them.

By late afternoon, feeling a bit calmer, I began analyzing the situation and realized that perhaps I wasn't satisfying her anymore with my way of loving, or maybe she had an emotional disorder or even a physiological disorder that had intensified during our relationship. So, I thought of advising her to get a medical check-up. I waited for her to show up at my apartment that night.

I waited for many hours, though I didn't stop studying what I needed to. She didn't show up, probably wanting me to feel guilty about what I had said and begging her to accept her desires, which meant I would have to wait a long time, as I didn't follow that mantra.

The week passed, and whenever she ran into me, she tried to avoid me by all means. I continued with my studies, aiming to learn something new every day. It was my main goal. It would also be good for us to take time to define our feelings and continue our relationship with new vigor or go our separate ways.

Four weeks went by, and I had almost forgotten about her. On the contrary, I was glad to end a toxic relationship and dedicate my time to something more objective. I had started running in the mornings and swimming in the afternoons or on weekends. My skin had a natural tan, and my athletic posture was more noticeable and perhaps more appealing to the opposite sex. Hence, more girls tried to get close to me, awakening in her the desire she had kept latent in her mind and wanted to unleash with her body.

So, that night around eight, she showed up at my door, jokingly pretending to be a delivery person calling out, 'Pizza time!' Confused upon opening the door, I said, 'You've got the wrong place, I didn't order any pizza.' But upon realizing who was knocking, I ended up laughing and invited her in. Amidst laughter and handshakes, we ended up embracing each other with a strong and passionate kiss that erased all the disagreements that might have existed during the days of separation, driven by misunderstanding or any other reason.

We didn't have time to give explanations; on the contrary, that interval . The time without sexual activity had served to charge "Our young bodies charged with adrenaline, causing our hearts to beat at a rapid pace, leading us to lose our minds at the touch of our bodies. Laden with static from the friction of our caresses, igniting mutual desire with the release of our pheromones, and the yearning to fertilize each other with our reproductive fluids starting to flow in torrents, urgently seeking an immediate receptor. With no time to reach the bedroom, we sprawled on the living room carpet and unleashed our repressed impulses.

Without her asking me, I began to tighten her throat, little by little, as I tightened it more... I felt those contractions that produced an inexpressible sensation, and I continued squeezing without thinking about anything, only about the delirium that her contractions caused me. Suddenly everything stopped, no more response to my movements, no more satisfied moans from her. It was then that I reacted and realized that she was in a state of complete relaxation, her eyes extremely wide open, her limbs limp, inert, and without any motor reaction.

I panicked, suddenly all the lust had turned into panic, into fear of the predictable, as I knew in advance the consequences of our reckless actions. It was time to discover the extent of the damage, to know if it was reparable or if it was irreparable. Immediately, by instinct or logical consequence, I lifted her slightly, supporting my hand on her nape, blew on her beautiful face, and tried to move her arms to activate her blood circulation. Nothing... I gave her mouth-to-mouth resuscitation... and nothing. I felt fear and thought of calling 911, but I was more afraid to think that I was responsible for her death, that my entire future would go down the drain, and that I would spend a long time in jail. I insisted on reviving her and gave her cardiac massage, but it wasn't enough. Unfortunately, she had passed away, a victim of asphyxiation and something else, but the truth was: once again, I had become a murderer, a passionate murderer, but it didn't matter. I was a true monster, paying with death those who tried to love me and give me their all.

Now what worried me most was how I would get rid of such a beautiful corpse. I knew my DNA was all over her body, from her delicious mouth, the one I would never kiss again, to her body, where I left the sweat that emanated in the heat of our passion, to her sex, which carried all my virility, to her hair, which carried the cells of my hands that caressed her tenderly and would never do so again. I sat on the sofa, wanting to clear my mind, wanting to think about how to erase any trace and anything that could link her to me if she were found. I kept thinking for at least an hour; I had to devise an infallible plan... And the answer to my questions came. I had found the solution to my problem; the same fears I had the first time and the same solution would be what I put into practice. Nature would be the one to erase any traces, and all I would do after carrying out my plan would be to pray for her soul and keep the beautiful memories of what we had lived through.

I waited until midnight had passed, recalling the places I was going to run to. There was a stone under some bushes, long and flat, and I was sure that with my strength and a suitable lever, I could move it. So, I took the keys to her car after putting on her clothes and shoes. Just like the previous time, I took her by the waist, pretending she was drunk (in case someone saw us). We walked to her car parked on the street, and I placed her in the back seat. Then, stealthily, I searched the gardener's tool shed for something that could serve as a lever to move the stone I had in mind. I found a small shovel and an iron bar that would serve their purpose well, and I headed to the mentioned recreation area.

Everything was in semi-darkness, only the sound of crickets and any nocturnal birds or animals could be heard, recreating or feeding. With the lights off, I approached as much as I could and began my tough task. With a little effort due to my strong build, I managed to turn the huge stone, leaving an imprint resembling a grave. Then, I started digging as fast as I could, as if someone might appear and catch me. I think it was my guilt complex that made me hurry, but nevertheless, I managed to dig a hole about a meter and a half deep. Next, I went for the lifeless body of what was once a beautiful and tender woman and placed it in the dug space. I then started to fill it with soil, which I took special care to compress firmly. After putting the majority of the soil, I placed the stone back in its place and evenly watered the remaining soil so that it wouldn't be noticeable. The light drizzle that fell would ensure that everything appeared undisturbed, as if nothing had happened. Only I knew that a good woman would rest there forever, who was in the wrong place at the wrong time.

The only thing left was to get rid of the car, another tense moment, but I knew I would succeed. Nothing stood in the way of my plans; it had always been that way, and this time would be no exception to the rule. So, I drove the same car to a boat dumping site, where there was a steep slope along the shore. After wiping away any traces of mine, I gently slid it into the water, where it began to sink slowly, under an immense bubbling that marked the end of a stressful but satisfying conclusion. I had thrown the tools into the deep waters, and wearing sportswear, I ran back as I did during my exercise hours. As always, news of her disappearance was broadcast on television until after seventy-two hours. Numerous hypotheses were presented, but only I knew that she was in a better place than many in this world. I only hoped that her sins had been forgiven, which I would pray for in my occasional prayers.

Chapter VI

I wasn't sure if I had become a cynic, someone overly confident, or someone betting on luck. But what I was certain of was that I had become a silent killer, whether by chance or bad luck. Although I still felt a sense of guilt, I had started feeling an additional sentiment - resentment towards part of society. How was it possible for two young women with bright futures to pass away? Whatever the reason, it wasn't justified, as others who were a burden to society, no matter how you looked at it, roamed around, wandering like zombies, numbing themselves with anything that served that purpose, paying with whatever currency they received, be it money, sex, or anything that could be bartered for the purpose. Men or women who practically lived anywhere in the city, using public spaces to sleep at any hour of the day or night, to tend to their physiological needs, or even engage in sexual acts, presenting a deplorable image for citizens, whether they be children, women, or the elderly. They were a depressing example for everyone in general, not to mention the breeding ground for infections and subsequent diseases.

Though there were certain kinds of people I tried to help, motivated by the memory of my mentor 'Daniel', who had been a vagabond for a part of his life, although I only considered them based on their age, as they might have been individuals forgotten by their families

- be it their children, spouses, etc. But there was one night when I felt such compassion for the situation they lived in that I undertook the absurd task of relieving them of so much suffering... and I began to conceive a way, in a somewhat compassionate manner, as my idea was for them not to suffer at all in leaving this world of the living, to move on to the realm where they no longer suffer, neither in mind nor body, to rescue them from their daily suffering, facing the depressing appearance they had acquired and the hardships they went through just to numb themselves, to stop thinking about the same things, at least until they felt the need to seek it again and resume their torment.

There was a little street I had to pass through to reach my apartment, where at least six or eight of the homeless wandered and asked anyone who crossed their path. There was also a poor woman around forty years old; I felt pity for the waste of her beauty, as traces of her beautiful face and the remnants of her once-beautiful body remained. I went into a liquor store and bought a small bottle of liquor. I noticed they were selling sleeping pills, and an idea came to mind to offer the opened bottle to see their reaction. The lady accepted it without a word and drank it in one go. When she had consumed half, she managed to say thank you before finishing the rest of the bottle.

I had found a way to relieve the suffering of those who it might apply to, so the next day I would set my plan in motion. At this point, I didn't care if I were to be condemned one day for killing two, four, or more. The first in my plans was the former beautiful woman. It occurred to me that perhaps she was suffering from her infidelity, seeking to atone for her guilt in such an aberrant manner. I intended to put an end to it, to prevent her from continuing to set a bad example, from consuming herself gradually without finding relief for her sorrows, attempting to erase her misdeeds by adding more that made her feel worse than when she committed her sin. I would be the relief to her despair, I would help her find a merciful death, assist her in reaching her settlement with the Creator, to stop suffering in this world where we pay for everything we've done. Because nearly everyone regrets their sins when they die, thus we won't have to pay anything in the other world, as God will surely forgive us as a reward for our repentance.

That night, I studied until late, preparing for end-of-term exams for the second year of my law degree. I read about reduced sentences for confessing crimes. It occurred to me that if I confessed what had happened with my two loves, I might get a favorable trial, and perhaps, if I could prove that it was all accidental, I might not even have to go to jail. Upon careful consideration, I found within myself a solution to my emotional problems. I discovered something I didn't know existed in me: my fear of God. It was innate, as my parents took me to church very few times, but I realized there was a connection. He had looked after me for a long time, and what had happened to me was circumstantial; it wasn't that I was a criminal. I had been involved in two different accidents, and I wasn't a hundred percent guilty.

The next day, instead of giving the adulterated liquor to the beautiful lady, I opted to buy her a delicious breakfast and a refreshing drink to hydrate her. I tried to engage in small talk to understand the reason for her determination in that life. She wasn't very communicative, but I could see a hint of gratitude in her eyes and the sorrow of being in front of a handsome man in her ragged and filthy appearance. I asked, 'Where do you sleep?' She replied, 'Wherever night catches me!' I knew my budget was limited, as I lived on what Mr. Bill sent me every month. However, considering she had no vices and being very methodical with my expenses, I had a small savings fund that I thought of using to offer some help. But it felt too soon, as she didn't know me and might have been suspicious. So, I promised her I'd see her the next day and encouraged her to avoid alcohol by all means.

I said goodbye and continued my way to the study center, thinking about the healthiest way to help her without offending or committing too much. I wanted to gift her a dress and perhaps some undergarments, but I wasn't sure if that would bother her or if it would be appropriate. However, after leaving the exam room, I had the chance encounter with a student who bore a striking resemblance in appearance to the beautiful lady. Abruptly, I asked her, leaving her bewildered:

'What dress size do you wear?' She replied somewhat embarrassed, 'Why do you want to know? It would be lengthy to explain.' 'Would you mind if I asked you a favor, provided you're not busy and willing to help me?' I said. She responded, 'I have a couple of hours before I get home, and if it's not something bad or dangerous, of course, I'd like to help.'

Come... I'll explain on the way. My name is Alexis Smith Siemens, and I'm finishing my second year of Law. What about you?' 'My name is Barbara, I'm in my first year in the same career as you. Tell me, how was your first year?' 'Do you want the truth? It went well, just like this year. It all depends on how determined you are to move forward and graduate. Always set goals to know where you stand, and the main thing is to have the desire to succeed.' 'I forgot to mention I don't have a car, so we'll have to take the bus, does that bother you?' She replied, 'Of course not, I'll give you a ride in my car.' As we got into her car, I said, 'The truth is, I want to help a woman living on the street who worries me, not only for her homeless situation but also for the fact that she's a woman. I thought about buying her a dress and some undergarments, and perhaps taking her to a place for a bath, so she can feel important again, or at least know that someone cares about her situation.'

'I can see you're a person with a good heart,' she said, 'as very few people are nowadays. So, not only will I help you buy that dress and everything else, but I'll come with you so she won't feel embarrassed by your gift, and we'll find a place for her to rest and have a decent meal. I'll pay for the gas,' I said, but she replied, 'Don't even mention it; let me be part of your charitable work.' And we headed to a store to find what we were looking for. After finding the store and selecting what we wanted, she insisted on paying half of the amount, even though I hesitated.

We set off again to the place where we might find the lady in question, but she wasn't there. However, my instinct suggested we take a stroll around the block, so when we arrived at the next corner, I spotted the beautiful, dusty lady eating something wrapped in a paper bag. We approached her and offered her to come with us, and the first thing that came to my mind was to go to my apartment, where I hoped we could make a transformation.

We didn't take long to arrive, although the lady hesitated a lot before getting into the car. Eventually, she had no argument not to. Upon arriving, I politely asked her to come in, then handed her a plastic bag to put the clothes she would take off before taking a warm bath, and gave her the new clothing along with a scented liquid soap for women. 'Why are you doing this?' asked the bewildered lady. 'For humanitarian reasons,' I said, 'so don't worry about taking your time to bathe. We want you to thoroughly enjoy the beginning of your new life.' In the meantime, I asked my newly met friend to sit down and offered her a drink, while also taking some vegetables and chicken pieces from the refrigerator to cook. 'What are you going to do?' she asked, as she stood up and said, 'I'll help you prepare dinner. It should have a feminine touch to taste better,' she boasted.

Due to the length of the text provided, I'll proceed with the translation in parts to ensure accuracy and continuity.

After taking a prolonged bath for almost half an hour, she emerged refreshed and brimming with satisfaction. Her appearance was very flattering. I asked Barbara to help dry her hair and apply some cream or something to enhance her appearance. Barbara didn't hold back; on the contrary, she gifted her a lipstick and a box of something called 'powder blush,' which radically changed her appearance, revealing the natural beauty I had observed in her earlier. Then, we invited her to sit at the table and share the delicious chicken dinner Barbara and I had prepared together.

While we dined, I analyzed her qualities as a person. I realized she was cultured; she never used any vulgar terms during our conversation. Moreover, she had good manners in using the eating utensils. We enjoyed dinner as if we were a family. I felt she needed that familial communication, just like me, and perhaps my new friend who had automatically joined my purpose, which had unexpectedly begun. After dinner, I took charge of preparing a delicious and aromatic coffee (while Barbara cleared the table), which would complement the chocolate chip cookies and serve as a prelude to learn more about the reason behind the waste of the beautiful lady's life.

She insisted on clearing the table and washing the used utensils. However, I warned her that she was our guest, so she shouldn't insist on it. Instead, she should get used to enjoying the evening, which would be a bit long. While we enjoyed the delightful coffee, I tried to ask her, being very discreet in my approach: 'What was the reason for you wasting your life like this?' Hiding her face in her hands, she burst into tears and cried for a few minutes. Her crying made our silence as heavy as lead. After interrupting her crying, she said, 'I haven't been a good mother or a good wife, and I thought I had to pay for the damage I caused to my family, which fell apart due to my infidelity and lack of sanity. But I think I've suffered enough and will try to organize my life, to be someone different from what I was for some time. Thank you for giving me the inspiration and the initial help; from now on, I'll try to leave that miserable life behind.'

I felt like crying. I felt it was the story of my home, and I thought I wouldn't want it to be my mother who had to pay for the harm she caused me and my father, who lovingly trusted her. Although everyone is responsible for their actions and as a culprit must pay for them, deep down, I believe destiny had prepared compensation for my own sufferings. Life, in return, had given me the opportunity to become stronger and adapt to circumstances, achieving what I am now and surely what she would achieve too.

After calming her down, I asked her to please stay in my apartment, suggesting that I'd sleep in the living room and that she should take care of keeping everything tidy, with Barbara as her advisor. When she felt better, we would try to guide her life to another level. Barbara agreed and promised to visit her every day, to be her counselor and shoulder to cry on if necessary. 'I knew God would take pity on me,' she said, 'that all my sufferings and tears of remorse would be a sign of my desire to be a different person. He put a couple of angels in my path to rescue me from that hell I turned my life into due to my mistakes.' 'Well, I'll leave you alone,' I said, heading to the bedroom to get what I needed to sleep and dress for the next day to go to the study center.

I woke up early as usual, took my morning shower, and after preparing coffee and a sandwich, which I had for breakfast, I headed to the study center. Barbara was waiting for me at the student center door; her gaze showed how excited she was and how eager she was to ask me questions. 'Hi, Alexis, how was it with your guest? Did she behave well and go to bed early?' 'Hi,

Barbara, yes, she went to bed as soon as you left; she just brushed her teeth with her new toothbrush, which was your smart idea to buy. I want to thank you for trusting me so much. I know you don't know me at all, yet you cooperated with me all the time. I anticipate that anytime you need anything, I'll be ready to help you unconditionally. You can ask for anything, and I'll be there.' 'What do you say if you take me dancing one of these nights?' She chuckled, 'Don't worry, I was just testing you.' 'Done,' I replied, 'as soon as the exams are over, I'll let you know. See you after class!' And I hurried to arrive on time for the exam scheduled for that day.

I didn't lose focus during the exams, but as soon as I left the classroom, I had a niggling question in my mind: Why do I feel this special affection for an older and unknown woman? Could it be that I feel sorry for what happened to the two beautiful departed women, or is it my humanitarian spirit that drives me? Well, whatever it was, it made me feel good about myself, and that was the most important thing.

Upon leaving the student center, Barbara was already waiting at the entrance. It seemed as if she could read my mind and knew all my movements in advance. I felt a bit uncomfortable with that; I sensed as if suddenly she could read my thoughts and discover what had happened with my two loves. But my logic helped dispel my fears; there's still no one who can read anyone's mind, except the Almighty, who knows what we do and don't do. So, I felt a bit more secure and headed toward her, greeting her more attentively. 'How was your day?' I asked. She replied, 'Very good, you know, we'll have exams next week. Initially, I was scared, but now that you're around, I know you'll help me prepare in the best way possible to ace them.' 'Of course, you know you can count on that,' I said.

I wouldn't want you to incur expenses that aren't in your budget, so I'm not asking you to go to my apartment, although I know it would be very helpful for Jenny if you visited her from time to time.' 'Don't worry, I know exactly how much I can spend, and I'm not too concerned because if I ever face any trouble, I'm sure my dad wouldn't deny me his help, especially when it comes to an act of altruism.'

I remind you again,' I said, 'that since yesterday, my promise stands: anything I can do for you, consider it done. I'll also help you achieve your best grades, even if my help is just a supplement, because you're a very intelligent woman with talent to succeed even without my help.' 'I know you're very gallant,' she replied, 'but there's never any harm in the help of someone who has more experience than oneself, especially someone like you, who is an excellent student. I saw you're on the honor roll; congratulations.'

We walked to her car and headed to my place. Upon arrival, we were greeted by Jenny, who was in the middle of cleaning the apartment. There was also a delicious smell of homemade food; she had prepared a delightful chicken stew and immediately asked us to sit down, serving the exquisite meal. Of course, Barbara didn't just sit and wait; on the contrary, she helped serve the delicious food, and the three of us sat down at the table. We didn't have time to say anything until we enjoyed the exquisite menu, which made my imagination fly back to my subconscious, where I still retained the taste and aroma of the food my mother used to prepare when I was a child. It was curious and inquisitive, reminding me vaguely of my mother, and I felt a special fondness for her. However, I was afraid to ask her any questions that might jeopardize the closeness I had achieved with her, so I thought I'd give it time.

After such a succulent meal, we sat down to watch some television and discuss unimportant things while preparing the topics Barbara would have to study for the exams the following week. Surprisingly, it occurred to me to ask Jenny which state she was from. She hesitated for a moment, and after a few seconds, she said, 'I was born in North Carolina, and I recently moved to Florida due to the twists of fate. I fell into drinking, but thankfully, I had the good fortune of finding you and here I am, trying to correct my course and be better than before after experiencing the dark side of life.'

The three of us started a new routine. Jenny, who had already become familiar with us, had started going to the store and other places to buy things needed for the house. Barbara came every afternoon to eat with us and study a little in her respective area, and I tried to stay in touch with Mr. Bill to keep the financial aid secure, which was crucial for my purposes. With Doris, I talked very occasionally, and she continued with her same arrogant and pretentious attitude, so our conversations were just greetings and goodbyes. I had started to notice Barbara's physical qualities because initially, I was so concerned that I had only noticed her humanitarian talents, her generosity, and altruism.

"One afternoon, while Jenny and Barbara were talking, I noticed the slender figure of the young woman. She was as tall as Jenny, about five-ten, with brown hair, almond-shaped eyes. Her face had a small, straight nose, and her red, well-defined lips adorned with white, perfect teeth formed a beautiful smile. Long, curved lashes adorned her large eyes, complementing her well-defined eyebrows. Under her long hair hid a pair of pretty, small ears, and her long, smooth neck led to her feminine shoulders. She had ample, solid breasts, wide hips, and long, well-shaped legs. Her slightly bronzed skin tone from the tropical sun gave her the appearance of a princess from an Equatorial Island.

I thought I was falling in love again, and I was scared, very scared because the two times I had the chance to venture into love, I ended up hurt and traumatized. I didn't want something so painful to happen to me again. I didn't want to end someone else's dreams and ambitions, especially not the life of such a beautiful and good woman...

The three of us had become accustomed to our relationship, just like Dumas' novel 'The Three Musketeers,' one for all and all for one. We laughed, talked about everything, except anything related to Jenny's mysterious background, or mine, as I didn't want my painful past to be known. However, Barbara told us everything about her wealthy family from North Texas, and I formed a very good impression and concept about them.

One of those afternoons when Barbara and I returned, we found a small letter on the dining table. It had elegant handwriting and said: 'Please don't judge me. I know this isn't the right way to leave, but it was necessary. Otherwise, I'm sure you would have convinced me to stay, and I wouldn't have been able to resist the words of two exceptional beings like you. I know you care for each other, and three people don't make a couple. I also want you to know that, in gratitude for your kindness, I won't approach alcohol again. From now on, I'll dedicate my life to worthy purposes for the benefit of others. I love you... Jenny. P.S. Don't look for me because by the time you read these lines, I'll be far away.'

I felt dismayed by the news. Barbara didn't say anything; I was just surprised to see her beautiful eyes fill with tears as she clutched the small letter to her chest, whispering softly, almost inaudibly... 'May God be with you, Jenny. We will miss you.' Suddenly, she embraced my chest, seeking refuge for her sadness, and then she cried as much as she could. She clung to me desperately, and after long minutes, when she was finally calm, she asked me to join her in a prayer, wishing the best for such a sweet and suffering woman.

That was a long night. After the tears came the joy of memories and the satisfaction of what we had done for the beautiful woman. We knew we couldn't do anything more, just remember her fondly and wish her the best in her new project. But there was a question lingering in the air... Was she right about Barbara and me being in love? Would she guess it or was it too obvious from our affection at all times? Anyway, it's a night after so much sadness and a burst of joy. I asked Barbara to be my girlfriend... if there were no obstacles, of course. There's nothing stopping us from being happy (she said), and we sealed the commitment of a long love relationship with a tender and passionate kiss, sublime and pure, as we didn't want to taint the memory of a beloved person.

She slept in my apartment, in the same bed that Jenny once occupied. The next day, when Barbara woke up, she asked me what clothes I would wear to go to the study center. She was surprised to find my primary school ID card on the drawer, the only thing I kept with me after so long. She asked, 'Why does this card say your name is Alexis Smith?' 'It's a long story, and I'd prefer to tell you about it in the future. But I assure you that you'll know in due time,' I said. However, a question started brewing in my mind that defied logic... What connection could the ID card have with Jenny's departure? It seemed so odd that she would leave abruptly after finding it. Did something so insignificant disturb her memory? Well, I'd find a logical answer eventually. There was no rush.

We headed to the educational center to fill our minds with new knowledge, to forget the nostalgic while focusing on learning new things that would lay the foundation for our future. We forgot about everything; when we left classes, we didn't know what topic to discuss. As always, feminine delicacy broke the ice, suggesting we have dinner in the intimacy of my home and discuss what our relationship would be in the future. So, we went to my apartment and, to the rhythm of romantic orchestral music, we dined—or pretended to dine—without averting our gazes from each other, as if wanting to penetrate our souls without having to say a word to express what we felt inside, to express the hopes of two young hearts that could hardly contain the desire to love.

We finished dinner, leaving the plates almost the same as when we started eating. Our appetite was different; we wanted to taste the forbidden fruit, to satiate our bodies with something more substantial. Kissing has a different taste, depending on the intensity with which they are given and received. Although our passion desired more than just kisses, our bodies were charged with energy. When I brought her close to me, I felt a surge of who knows how many volts. My skin tingled, and the desire to possess her overwhelmed me—to hold her body against mine and make her tremble with emotion, to form a single mass with our bodies and merge our souls in an act of love.

I managed to suppress my emotion for a moment as I carried her in my strong arms, suspended in the air, and gently placed her on the bed. I kissed her passionately, tenderly, and as I kissed her, my animal instincts overflowed, and I began to remove, unhurriedly but at a good pace, each of her garments that hindered our desires. It was an amazing sight to see her naked body. I was astonished at the wonder that nature had conceived in that beautiful body. She could have been the envy of Venus or any mythological Goddess, indeed the envy of any mortal, for she seemed like an angel escaped from heaven materialized in that beautiful woman.

I behaved like a fool because, in my admiration of such a beautiful and delicate body, I forgot to quickly get rid of my clothes. Reacting to her pleading with feline-like moans, I literally tore off my clothes and positioned myself beside her to continue with such a delightful surrender. It was a delirious night, full of love and pleasure. I imagined her moans as the singing of the sirens in mythology, those whose songs drove men to madness, losing the reason that I had lost the moment my eyes met that delightful and angelic body. I don't know how many times we came together, but it felt insufficient, and I wanted more, and more, and more... until tiredness overtook us, and we had to surrender to the mandate of the God of sleep, the benevolent Morpheus who did not embrace us.

We woke up tired, exhausted, and worn out, trembling with weakness, but with an indescribable joy that gave our bodies the strength to stand, despite the overflow of emotions and energy. That day, we wouldn't do anything other than love each other, dream awake, delight in each other's observation of our young bodies, and overflow with desire to keep loving each other, to possess each other body and soul, to reach the sky with our hands at every moment of our magical encounters.

And so, the day passed and part of the night. We knew we had to return to reality, that we had all the time in the world to keep loving each other, but we needed to put our feet on the ground and continue with our purpose of building a good future, something with solid foundations that would be a platform to fulfill our youthful dreams. So, we had to rest to continue with our exciting and instructive routine.

We had connected in such a way that when I asked her something, it seemed she already knew her response in advance. So, we agreed to have a healthy relationship, to love each other platonically during the student weekdays, and to love each other wildly during the weekends, taking advantage to enjoy the sun, beach, and sports. And so

I hadn't been able to say anything; everything happened so fast. Besides, it was a family matter, and I trusted that I would soon know what it was about. Although I sensed that dark clouds were approaching our lives, something that would give a new direction to our relationship. A relationship that had helped dispel my fear of happiness, while also making me forget the traumatic incidents with the two beautiful women who had met the worst of fates.

I had waited until late at night, and I didn't know when I fell asleep on the couch. I was only awakened by the freshness of dawn and sensing that she wouldn't arrive, I decided to retire to the bedroom. Even though I had a restless dream, I managed to rest a bit. Continuing with my routine, I got up to head to the educational center, hoping to find her and learn more details about the situation, expecting a clear explanation and to know what was really happening.

As if my suffering were not enough, with the sure loss of that new love that had given my life a reason to hope, and the escape from memories that tormented my mind, the siege of memories that made me different from other men.

That afternoon, upon returning from university, I received a call from the Memorial Hospital in Miami, Florida, they needed my presence. They didn't clarify much, just that Jenny had asked for my presence to bid me farewell. 'Farewell?' It sounded strange and intriguing, but still, I promised to arrive as soon as possible. I couldn't say how long it took me to arrive, but I know it was fast. Upon arriving, I reported at the front desk and explained the reason for my visit. A very pretty and beautiful nurse led me to her presence. In the presence of Jenny, with a melodious and polite voice, she asked me to be brief and try not to excite or upset her, as she was in a delicate state of health.

With a soft and affectionate voice, I approached her. I didn't know what to say. Finally, after clearing my throat, I said, 'How do you feel, and what's the problem?' She answered in a subdued voice, 'I'm not well, I have terminal cancer, and it's metastasizing. My hours are numbered, but I wanted to say goodbye and also ask for your forgiveness for the harm I caused in your life. Although God has rewarded you with the company of good and affectionate people, who have compensated for the love I couldn't give you, the betrayal to your father didn't last long before he realized and forced me to leave home. That's when I fell into drinking, and God brought me close to you to enjoy your presence, even if it was for a while, and to have the chance to ask for forgiveness.' 'Mother, I have nothing to forgive you for, on the contrary, thank you for the lovely time you dedicated to me. Tell me what

I can do for you.' 'Nothing,' she said. 'Just forgive me, have a small religious service, and my Christian burial (if you can). You can count on it, Mother, but let me seek a second opinion.' 'Everything is confirmed, and it's most likely to happen today itself. Let me give you a kiss on the forehead and bless you, as I used to when you were just a child.' I couldn't contain my tears and sought refuge in her arms, feeling like the child who didn't want his mother to go, now that I had found her again.

The nurse, who had been observing the events, approached me with a Kleenex in her hand, while in the other, she held hers, wiping away the tears still streaming from her eyes. Both of us blushed and turned towards where my mother was lying in bed. Her arm that hung at the edge of the bed, where I had embraced her, hung inert, flaccid, and pale. The nurse hurried to check on her and urgently called the on-duty doctor. As she began CPR, the doctor appeared, taking charge of the situation. After what felt like hours but were only a few minutes, the doctor, with a furrowed brow and solemn words, said, 'I'm sorry, there's nothing to be done. Cancer has done its evil work. My heartfelt condolences... rest in peace.' The kind nurse also approached me, discreetly hugging me and still sobbing, said, 'I'm truly sorry. I know how much you loved each other. If you need help with the arrangements, count on me. She requested to be cremated.'

I approached her again, grasping her now limp and smooth hand, which still retained the warmth and scent of her skin, a fragrance that had been etched in my mental olfactory since I was a baby. I continued crying beside her for a while longer, until some nurses separated me from her. They kindly told me they needed to take her to the morgue, that if I wanted to keep vigil, I could see her for a longer time. After the arrangements, they took her to the funeral home where my great friend, father, and mentor had been. So many memories flowed through my mind, sweet memories of my tender childhood. I remembered the squirrels on the roof of our house, my tender little brother, who must be a grown man now, my mother cooking dinner and the delicious apple pie, my father, who, although tired from work, always found time to check my homework and read me a story while waiting for me to fall asleep, my mother always obsessed with my appearance and my cursed hairstyle. She combed my hair I don't know how many times until she thought it was okay.

To my mentor, who always cared that I kept my mind occupied, as he used to say that an idle mind can only think nonsense. That's why my addiction to knowledge, to learning new things every day, because there will always be a day when what you've learned will be useful. Was I lost in my thoughts that I hadn't noticed the presence of my Uncle and Cousin, which surprised me greatly, looking around as if trying to figure out where their deceased relative was. 'Don't worry,' said Uncle, 'we're here to support you through your loss. I know you loved her very much, despite not seeing her for many years. How did we know? We were concerned about your safety and contacted the building manager, with the order to inform us of any emergency you might have. 'Only emergencies,' the rest of your life is private, and I know you'd never do anything reproachable... I guarantee it.' I thought, if he knew about the two girls, he might drop dead or distance himself from me as if I were a rabid dog. Suddenly he asked, 'Where will she be buried?' I replied like a robot: 'She'll be cremated, it was her wish, and that's what she requested at the hospital admission.' Uncle said, 'I find it inhumane to burn a human being, but if it was her decision, it must be respected.'

My cousin hadn't said anything, but when Uncle stopped talking, she stood by my side and gave me a strong hug that made every membrane in my body vibrate, and then she said in a soft, melodious, and captivating voice, 'My sincere condolences, cousin. Count on us for whatever you need.'

They stayed with me for most of the night, and when I saw Doris nodding off, I asked Uncle Bill to leave, saying that I would be okay and that I greatly appreciated their consideration. They said goodbye again with a hug, and Doris also gave me a discreet but warm and expressive kiss. I felt in the kiss her support in my pain and her appreciation for my courage in the difficult moments I had faced, this... now for the second time.

The mourning passed, and I returned to classes. Now I had my mother's blessing, which was the last and greatest gift she gave me in life, and I knew that this blessing would be the extra boost that would help me succeed in my purpose.

I continued studying with more diligence; I read books as if reading the newspaper (hypothetical situation). Weeks, months, and years passed, and I didn't have any communication with Barbara or any other girl. I didn't want my heart to be broken again or to lose the compulsive illusion of being a good, no, the best lawyer in the State of Florida. There were several people who would be happy to see the fruit of my sacrifice and devotion: Daniel, my Mentor and Adoptive Father; my Mother (both from heaven); my Uncle Bill and Doris (here on earth); and my Father R R and Brother David, the latter to serve as my motivation.

Soon it would be the final exams, and I put extra effort into my thesis. I wanted it to be something very interesting, especially in self-defense, as many times people lose their cases by trusting lawyers with little experience or not knowing how to litigate the case, and they are convicted of crimes they might not have committed.

The awaited day arrived; I had passed the written exams, the private ones, and presented my thesis, which caused a lot of comments from the evaluators (the Senior Masters). In a few days, the graduation ceremony would take place. I was very excited and saddened not to have anyone with whom I could celebrate my joy, share my emotions. Barbara wasn't there, nor anyone interested in my triumph and my future expectations. Well, I would have time to celebrate by putting my knowledge at the service of those who needed it most.

And the day came. One by one, they were called by name to receive their diplomas until I heard my name... Alexis Smith Siemens, 'the lawyer,' I thought, and hurried to collect my diploma. I couldn't repeat what the person handing it to me said because I wasn't paying attention, busy looking for Barbara in all the seats of the audience. I was so focused on her that I didn't notice the presence of Uncle Bill and Doris until I almost tripped over them while trying to find a seat to keep watching the events unfold.

It was Uncle Bill who broke my stupor with his warm and effusive greeting and congratulations, to which I responded with gratitude after overcoming my emotional lethargy. 'Don't ignore me,' said Doris, 'I also want to congratulate you,' and gave me an intense hug, transmitting all her energy, making every cell in my body vibrate. She finished the hug with a 'congratulations,' with that melodious and rhythmic voice that made me stutter helplessly. 'After the ceremony, we'll go celebrate your success, young man,' said Uncle Bill. 'I made reservations at the best restaurant and bar in the city. There we'll also talk about your future in my law firm, plus something important I want to discuss with you.'

After the graduation ceremony, we headed to his car (a Bentley from that year), where his chauffeur was waiting for us. He attentively opened the door for Uncle Bill, and I did the same to let Doris in. She was elegantly dressed in a light-colored suit, a tailored style that accentuated her exquisite figure. We sat in the back, while Uncle sat in the front and gave instructions to the driver to head to the restaurant called Komodo or something like that. The driver dropped us off at the entrance and went to the valet parking to wait for the group.

I was dazzled by the beauty and luxury of the place. Fortunately, I was dressed in a nice suit I bought for the occasion, nothing compared to Uncle's or my elegant cousin Doris's attire, but it didn't stand out too much. My cousin escorted me, whispering in my ear, "This will be your way of life from now on. You'll start meeting important people, handling black credit cards, and constantly traveling to courts in different states to defend famous and wealthy clients." I felt confused by the 180-degree turn my life had taken in the last three or four hours. I felt like I was on cloud nine and couldn't fully react. While seated with the menu in hand, Uncle Bill dropped another bombshell, which completely sunk me into my seat—I felt like I was levitating. I was in a daze, feeling like it was all a dream until Doris woke me up with her melodious and suggestive voice. "Don't wake up yet," she said. "Dad hasn't finished. The best is yet to come." Uncle continued, "My dear nephew, you've earned my affection and respect for your learning ability, common sense, and the nobility of your heart. I believe you have all the potential to be an outstanding litigator and defender of just causes." He continued speaking, mentioning the hiring document for my law firm, starting with a good base salary and later a percentage of fees from cases won or lost. He also handed over the inheritance left by my brother, given on the condition of graduating from university first. He gave me the documents to deposit in an account or invest, advising me to consult his stockbroker. I asked him to keep the documents as I planned to visit his office in a few days to finalize everything. We continued enjoying the exquisite dinner, finishing with dessert and a delicious cup of coffee. Afterward, we headed to the car, heading towards my home. We sat in the same seats, Uncle nodding off, and we were silent, not knowing what to say. Suddenly, he took my hand with his delicate and perfumed hand, looked into my eyes, and slowly brought his lips close to mine, imprinting a tender and passionate kiss that made every cell in my body vibrate. After separating his tender and well-drawn lips from mine, I asked, "Didn't you hate me?" "No, silly," she replied. "My uncle noticed our mutual attraction and asked me to promise not to be an obstacle for you to achieve your goal. So I worked hard to prove the opposite of my feelings... and I succeeded, didn't I?

Chapter VII

It was another night where sleep evaded me. Thoughts raced through my mind like the bubbling waters of a hot spring. I was convinced I wasn't the ruthless murderer people might think. I decided I would speak with the prosecutor in a criminal court, request some concessions, and the promise of a reduced sentence in case I was found guilty.

Morning came, a cloudy and monotonous day. I grabbed my books containing articles of law that granted the right to self-defense, allowed exhumation for autopsy, and reduced sentences for confession of facts, but not guilt.

I leaped out of bed, took a cold shower to feel refreshed, grabbed my documents, and headed to the court I had chosen based on the county I lived in. Finally, I'd put a dent in my "new" title of criminal lawyer and prove what the son of two parents, R R and Daniel Siemens, was made of—the young lawyer in whom some people had placed all their trust and good wishes.

Arriving at the court, I went to the prosecutor's office, and after talking with him, we proceeded to the judge's office. Judge Thompson was a stout African-American man with a tiny mustache, a sonorous but kind voice. The prosecutor, Trenton, a blond man with a square-jawed face (he reminded me of Dick Tracy comics) had deep, inquisitive blue eyes and a deep voice with a possibly German or European accent, which sent shivers down my spine, perhaps due to my guilt complex.

After our meeting and completing certain documents relevant to the situation, the exhumation of Diana, my second victim, was ordered, just like Janet's, and consequently, their respective autopsies. Given my confession as a lawyer, I was placed under house arrest with an electronic ankle monitor—not so bad, considering I could have been held in jail and unable to prepare my defense. I was given three days to appear in court for the trial against me for the crimes of involuntary double homicide, evidence tampering, and mishandling of two corpses. It wasn't a race against time; with all the calm in the world, I filled out my official statement and the mitigating circumstances I believed would absolve me of guilt, thus clearing my reputation and my name, which I never wanted to tarnish for the memory of my father, mentor, and friend.

Llegó the moment of truth. At ten in the morning, I was seated in the defendant's dock. The announcer said in a loud voice: "The honorable Judge has arrived. All rise." We all stood up, the Judge appeared, and before taking his seat, he said, "You may be seated."

He began reading the papers on his desk, and his name could be seen on the wall above: "Judge" and below it,

"Hakim Thompson." He started his speech, stating, "We're here to prove the innocence or guilt of Alexis Smith Siemens for the crimes of involuntary manslaughter and mishandling of corpses. The floor is now yours, Prosecutor John Trenton."

And so began the accusation and presentation of evidence. "I conclude, Your Honor," said Trenton.

The defense or the accused may speak; in this case, it's the same person who has chosen to represent themselves," stated the judge.

It was my turn to present the cases. Though they were entirely different, they had the same tragic ending. "Your Honor, I'd like to present some documents that prove the predisposition of the two individuals detailed in your case history to die at any moment, if you allow?" The Judge responded affirmatively. As I approached and placed the documents on the stand, the Judge began reading them eagerly. Moments later, he said, "Proceed with your defense." I wanted to be brief and concise. "Miss Janet had a high alcohol concentration in her body, as per the autopsy report. She also suffered from angina pectoris, certified by Doctor Prescott in her medical history. Additionally, a large amount of antifreeze was found in her body, leading police detectives to commence a thorough investigation as she was the sole heir to a substantial sum of money. Regarding the second deceased person, Miss Diana had a significant amount of cocaine in her body. Also, as per her medical history certified by Doctor Mathews, she suffered from a narrowed heart valve, leading to lower-than-usual oxygen levels. Combined, the excessive cocaine, the valve's condition, and the lack of oxygen due to her sexual extravagances resulted in a massive myocardial infarction causing her instantaneous death. As for my involvement, I was a student with many dreams, one of which was to become a lawyer. Good or bad, I don't know. I thought if the police arrived, I could be charged with homicide, murder, or I didn't know what. But now, I realize it was just being in the wrong place at the wrong time. Now we must await the jury's decision and Your Honor's sentence... I have concluded."

I hadn't looked behind me as my attention was on the Judge and the Prosecutor. Instinctively, I turned around and was surprised to see Uncle Bill and Doris. I felt tremendous embarrassment seeing Doris; I think I turned red as a tomato. I wished the earth would swallow me, but there was nothing to be done. Uncle Bill nodded, and Doris raised her hand in a shy hello. The court adjourned as the jury deliberated.

An hour later, the jury returned, and the Judge asked, "Have you reached a conclusion?" The representative responded, "Innocent of the charges of homicide, only responsible for mishandling corpses." The Judge declared, "This court finds Alexis Smith Siemens innocent of the charges of homicide. For the charge of mishandling corpses, this court imposes a penalty of..."

Everyone was in suspense, and absolute silence filled the room. "Two months of community service in this court," he said.

Everyone cheered for Alexis: "Long live," "Bravo," "Hurray!" Doris entered the room and hugged her life's love, saying, "You're magnificent." She was about to continue, but Uncle Bill interrupted, saying, "The debut of your title couldn't have been better. I'm proud of you, and what's done is done. Let's celebrate." Alexis apologized and went to sign some essential documents, then rejoined them. They left to celebrate at the same Komodo Restaurant. Uncle Bill, a very cautious man, had brought the job contract at his law firm and all concerning the inheritance left by Mentor Daniel, placing them on the table, one for signing and the other for banking deposits.

While eating, Uncle Bill mentioned something. "I knew you would come out well, so I called a journalist friend of mine and gave him the scoop on your case. Consequently, you'll be the talk of the day, starting tomorrow when you appear in the headlines as 'Lawyer of the Year.' Hahaha," and they continued eating and chatting enthusiastically.

After the meal and all the joy, the most tense moment of the afternoon arrived. Alexis, becoming serious, interrupted the laughter and comments, saying, "Uncle Bill, I hope you don't take this as presumption, but I can't keep my feelings to myself. I want to formally ask for Doris's hand. I believe she reciprocates what I feel, and if not, I think she'd say so immediately."

Uncle Bill immediately changed his amiable face and became serious, like Judge Thompson. Then, as if dragging the words, he asked Doris, "What do you have to say, my dear?

Here is the translation of the text to English:

Epilogue

Alexis and Doris got married; it was a lavish wedding, a celebration where Uncle Bill spared no expense. All the female guests admired the groom, and both young and old guests wondered, 'What a beautiful young lady! How did a stranger come and win such a beautiful woman and a good match at that?' The press didn't just limit themselves to writing compliments and good wishes for the brilliant lawyer Alexis Smith Siemens.

MORAL: This story contains a lot of truth based on the author's personal experiences and others that the author learned through confidences from some acquaintances and observations made throughout their life. By bringing together all these situations in this work, the goal was not only to offer an entertaining literary piece but also to impart a lesson for parents, spouses, and similar individuals to observe honesty in any romantic relationship, especially when teaching children. If we want emotionally healthy children, we must be discreet even in our behavior in intimacy with our partner. This is particularly crucial when we compromise the honor of our spouse, setting a bad example for our children. In cases like Alexis', it can cause significant trauma and numerous problems, especially emotional ones. Fortunately, in Alexis' case, he overcame it through his intelligence and the help provided by Daniel, his friend, mentor, and adoptive father. Conversely, it could have had a very different ending, similar to many adolescents who end up on the streets, without any purpose in life and immersed in drug addiction or other unfavorable circumstances.

END

www.ingramcontent.com/pod-product-compliance
Lightning Source LLC
Chambersburg PA
CBHW021554310726
48972CB00003B/817

* 9 7 8 1 9 6 3 3 2 9 4 3 8 *